With my best wishes

THE PHOTOGRAPHER'S FINAL EXPOSURE

Names, businesses etc. are fictional and the product of the authors imagination, whilst some of the characters are based on people the author knows or has known.

Text format and cover design by Mediaprint Solutions Limited.

PROLOGUE

The murder of professional photographer Arnold Frederick Dorsey had remained unsolved for some 10 years when a new cold case team is set up to review the file.

The team is headed up by DI Mike Morris who was due to retire but had agreed to take on this final unexpected job and put together just a small team to reinvestigate the case.

His choice of Billy Oliver and Dan Nichols came as some surprise to his DCI Geoff Gill, however having known these two aging pals and what their previous investigation experience had achieved, he agreed.

Billy Oliver was a retired Manchester PC, and his schoolboy pal Dan Nichols had spent his career in intelligence in the military.

The schoolboy friends had joined the army as teenagers on the same day but had been separated by their postings and had lost touch with each other for some 40 years.

Billy had left the Army and had joined the Manchester Police Force, and it wasn't until Dan also retired and decided to return to his native Manchester that the two old mates were reunited.

The Author's first novel

THE PHOTOGRAPHER'S FINAL EXPOSURE

CHAPTER 1

"Welcome to our new HQ Danny boy" Billy said as they both looked around the small storage room tucked away towards the back of the Police Station.

"Well at least it's got some furniture as well as a few storage shelves" he continued as he pointed to three old tired looking desks and chairs that looked like they'd been uncovered locked away somewhere else in the building and forgotten about for years.

"I think I prefer the Crown & Anchor" Dan said.

"Well, I guess we did do most of our best thinking there didn't we?" said Billy.

"Did you say thinking or drinking?" came the voice of DI Mike Morris who had just arrived at the open door.

"Get used to it lads, as this is all you are going to get, I am expecting the first of a few old case files to arrive any time" he continued leaving them alone, closing the door behind him.

The two old pals, Dan Nichols and Billy Oliver were still looking around, trying to envisage working together in this confined space, the reality of their new role as part of DI Mike Morris's newly chosen Police Cold Case Team finally sinking in.

Just then a gentle knock came at the door.

Billy answered, to see a young Asian chap standing there with 2 boxes in his arms. *"Is this the Review Team office?"* he said.

Dan and Billy looked at each other again realising that, yes it really is their office.

"Yes, that's right young fella" said Billy, "but we didn't order a takeaway".

"Shivi" the chap said, holding out a hand trying not to drop the boxes.

"What?" said Billy.

"Shivi, I was told to bring these old files for you" continued the young fella, almost apologising.

"Oh, right son, thanks" said Dan, moving over to take the boxes from him.

The young fella just stood there looking at Dan.

"Was there something else"? said Billy.

"I'm Shivi" repeated the young chap.

"Yes, you already told us that, are we supposed to tip you or something?" continued Billy.

"No, I'm Shivi" repeated the young man yet again, now looking decidedly uncomfortable.

Dan took over. *"Was there something else Shivi?".*

"Apart from your name that is" chirped in Billy.

"I was told to report here as your assistant" said Shivi, now looking a bit more confident and stretching a bit to peer into the room.

The two aging unlikely evidence men, now wondering what the hell they had let themselves in for by agreeing to Mike Morris's request to be part of this newly appointed cold case review team, looked at each other and said in unison, "assistant"?

"That's OK, we won't need an assistant, we can get our own coffee and stuff" Billy said, *"we can use the staff canteen here, but thanks anyway"* he continued, moving to close the door.

"No, I'm Shivi", repeated the lad yet again, now pushing his chest out just a little bit. "Your IT assistant"

"IT assistant"? the two old pals said together.

Mike Morris suddenly reappeared, now standing behind the young fella Shivi.

"I see the first of the cold case files have arrived lads, and you have met Shivindra, who will occupy this desk here" said Mike moving into the

room and pointing to the largest of the three old desks.

Mike turned and said, *"Now then Shivindra, all your computer equipment will be delivered today young man and will be set up for you to your liking, ready for our brand-new little unit to burst into action first thing tomorrow morning"* Mike said proudly.

Dan and Billy looked open mouthed at Mike.

"Shivindra is one of the brightest IT cadets from the Police College and will do all the research you lads will need, with all the very latest technology and equipment," said Mike.

"Er" began Billy, looking for some kind of further explanation, but before he had chance to say any more, Mike said *"OK, I will leave you three to get to know each other"*, and without a further word rushed off, closing the door behind him.

The young fella, who only looked about eighteen, stood looking up at his two aging team partners through big enquiring dark eyes, like an obedient puppy sat on the pavement edge waiting for the instruction to say when to cross the road. Dan's mind flashed back just for a second to his old neighbour Owen and his faithful golden retriever Brendan, poor Owen he thought.

After an awkward pause Dan eventually said, *"shall we all at least sit down then?"*.

Shivi immediately moved and sat by the big desk as if obeying an order, not noticing Billy's almost silent sigh and raised eyebrows.

After another short silence, Dan continued: *"How old are you Shivindra? I mean Shivi"*.

"I'm twenty-one, well I will be in four and a half weeks" he replied.

"So you are twenty" Billy said.

Dan immediately gave Billy one of those side glances as if to say, give the lad a chance.

"And what made you want to join the Police then" continued Dan.

"My dad was in the Army, and he sort of encouraged me to either join the military or the Police" replied Shivi.

"Well as you may have already been told, Billy here served in the Manchester Police, and I am from a military background. Billy and I have known each other from our school days here in Manchester. Where are you from then Shivi"? said Dan.

"Crumpsall" Shivi replied, feeling and looking a bit more comfortable.

"No, he means before that"? chipped in Billy, almost in interrogation mode.

By now it was quite noticeable that Shivi had a distinct local Manchester accent.

"Before that?" Shivi continued, *"Oh before that I lived in Lower Broughton".*

"No, where are you really from?" persisted Billy.

"Oh right, Shivi replied, *"I was born in Salford".*

Dan, now getting tired of Billy's irritating awkward questioning finally said. *"I have travelled quite a lot when I was in the military, and wondered where your family are originally from Shivi"?*

"Oh" replied Shivi, clearly oblivious to Billy's earlier attempts to try to make him feel awkward replied. *"My grandparents are from India; my grandfather was in the Army in India and fought for Great Britain in the war and my dad has all his medals".*

Now trying to make the lad feel a little more relaxed Dan said, *"Well I can tell you that I spent a little time in India, in New Delhi actually, where I met some great Indian military colleagues and their families who I still consider to be friends. When time allowed, they even took me to Agra to see the Taj Mahal".*

"Really?" said Shivi, clearly impressed and feeling more comfortable, *"I have never been to India, but I will do one day, I'm sure. Wow, and the Taj Mahal".*

Billy turned away and rolled his eyes a little.

Another knock at the door saw two men carrying what appeared to be a cartload of technical things, computer screens, wires, headphones and things neither Dan nor Billy had ever seen before.

"Where do you want your set up Shivi" one asked.

"This is my workstation here" he replied, pointing to the big desk area.

"Workstation?" Billy silently mouthed to Dan.

It was clear the two technical fellas already knew Shivi but didn't have a clue who Billy and Dan were, and totally ignored them both whilst chattering away setting up the IT equipment.

"Well, I suppose we should choose our workstations now Sherlock" Billy said sarcastically as they each picked up a box containing the old case files.

Over the next two hours Shivi and his two IT colleagues continued with their task, whilst Dan and Billy each sat at their workstations looking at the contents of the two boxes.

To the annoyance of everyone, the old swivel chair Billy had chosen made a loud squeak each time he even half turned, and Dan knew after a while Billy being Billy was doing it on purpose pretending not to look up.

The two old pals had been tasked by their new boss DI Mike Morris to go through the unsolved murder case relating to 46-year-old professional photographer Arnold Frederick Dorsey, who had been found battered to death in his studio in Manchester ten years before. Despite the best efforts of the Police at the time, no one was ever arrested, and no persons of interest had been established.

The boxes included all original statements taken by the investigating officers of the day, the crime scene photographic coverage, and all information considered relevant to the case including postmortem report as well as all Mr Dorsey's own medical records pre death.

Dan and Billy quickly found themselves now concentrating on the job in hand, looking through the documents. The plan was for them each to make notes and observations they felt they should discuss later with DI Mike Morris with a view to revisiting all area's that warranted further investigation.

Mr Dorsey's body was found on the studio floor in a pool of blood, his head and face had been severely beaten with one eye literally hanging out of its socket on a thread.

The vivid descriptive content of the information was so consuming that it was noticeable that Billy's chair had stopped squeaking, and the only distraction was from Shivi and his IT technicians chattering whilst still moving equipment and wires about around his "workstation".

"Do you want this monitor on this side?" asked one of the technicians. *"No, this side over here"* replied Shivi.

"OK, how's this then?" said the workstation chap after eventually moving the equipment. "That's tickety boo" replied Shivi in his broad Manchester accent.

Dan and Billy immediately raised their eyes from their desks and looked at each other for a second before returning to the documents.

After around another half hour the two technicians began tidying away their installation paraphernalia and finally said *"Well, how's that for you Shivi?* looking quite pleased with themselves.

"That's just tickety boo" replied Shivi with a final thumbs up.

Dan and Billy looked up again and silently mouthed to each other *"tickety boo"?*

CHAPTER 2

"Well, that was certainly a different day Danny boy" said Billy as they walked out of the Police Station after the first taste of their anticipated review team role and their new office. Not only that, but they also had a dedicated IT researcher assistant.

"You can say that again," said Dan. "What did you think about Shivi then?".

"Well to be honest, when he first arrived at the door and just kept saying Shivi, I thought he was sneezing, I thought he had a cold" replied Billy.

Dan laughed, never knowing whether Billy was joking or not.

"I guess we will have to get used to him. It seems strange, you just wouldn't expect such a local accent coming from somebody looking like Shivi would you?"

"Never mind that Danny boy, that poor young fella has got to get used to us two" said Billy as they continued walking along still chatting together about their day.

Without either of them really realising it, they were walking in the direction of the Crown & Anchor when they suddenly looked at each other and Billy said, *"What do you think Sherlock"*?

Dan replied with a broad smile, *"Why not eh?"*

Now sat at their usual table in their old HQ Dan said, *"The usual then is it Watson?"*

"Well, that would be just tickety boo Sherlock" replied Billy, and they both burst into laughter.

"Do you know Billy, when I decided to come back to Manchester after finally retiring, I naturally hoped we would meet up again, but I never dreamt we would end up getting involved in an official Police criminal cold case review team with Mike Morris."

"I know what you mean Dan" said Billy looking quite serious for a minute, *"I hope we are doing the right thing, I quite enjoyed combining our normal lifestyle with trying to get to the bottom of your neighbour's*

different problems, but let's not forget, we did uncover the conclusive evidence to resolve some serious issues didn't we, some of which led to convictions".

"But we just did our own thing following our instincts and bouncing ideas off each other, thinking outside the box I suppose, but this new role is obviously much different, and guidelines and procedures will have to be followed" continued Billy.

"Yes, I have some doubts about this new role as well" said Dan, *"but it'll be worse for you Billy, you have your open mike nights at the Golden Ball once a month, it's been a big part of your life, hasn't it?*

"No worries there Danny boy, I made that plain to Mike at the outset, my public need me" replied Billy, "so the first Friday of the month will continue as normal."

"Hey, just had a thought" said Dan, *"you really are Old Bill now. Do you get it Billy, Old Bill? you know, Police, Old Bill".*

"Leave the funnies to me Danny boy" Billy said as they finished off their drinks.

CHAPTER 3

The unfortunate demise of professional photographer Mr Dorsey a decade earlier lay heavy on the minds of both Dan and Billy as they each returned home and tried to settle in their own space for the evening.

Dan made himself a sandwich and sat in his favourite chair with a glass of red wine and put on some easy listening music on his old portable radio/CD player.

He started to mull over the content of the files he had been reading and tried to get a mental picture of the information that had already been established as factual, the pieces of the jigsaw they already had, and somehow, they now had to find the missing pieces.

He remembered it was always important to read witness statements not just once, but several times, as it can be easy to either misunderstand or mis interpret the actual meaning of the words. Peoples accents and different dialects when written down during statement taking can sometimes be misleading and sometimes just typing errors can infer a double meaning. How many times when struggling with the answer of a crossword, when the following day it's staring you in the face, and you wonder how I could have missed it the first time around.

His military duties involved travelling to several different countries and Dan recalled an occasion during his early training, attending a course where the speaker, a senior investigating officer relayed an occasion when he had received orders to attend the scene of a murder that had occurred on a ship at sea.

The report he received was that one of the kitchen staff had been cut in two by a Chinese chef with a meat cleaver. The officer explained his horror to the listening trainees of expecting to see a human body dismembered when he arrived at the scene, imagining this was probably some kind of old Chinese cultural act of revenge.

In the event the original information was that the victim had been *cut into* and not "cut in two" as it was copied in communications transit.

Dan also reminded himself of the old Chinese whispers quote of the WW1 soldier in the trenches who turned to his nearest comrade and said, *"Send reinforcements, we are going to advance".* The message was passed down the line, with the last message heard being: *"Send three and fourpence, we are going to a dance".*

Dan's second glass of wine helped convince him that this was where he was going to start the next day, check over all the statements again.

Just then the haunting song *"She"* by Charles Aznavour began to play.

Strange how a piece of music can instantly take one back to a place and time, even many years ago, even quicker than an email travels through cyberspace.

For that split moment Dan was back in Paris, chatting and having a glass of wine with the lovely Louise in the hotel bar. He couldn't believe that was 30 years ago.

Billy had called at the fish and chip shop on his way home from the Crown & Anchor.

As he continued on his way, he took the route by the old railway arches and passed by old Angus. Billy had known Angus from his PC days. Although locally classed as a tramp, a misfit, Angus was in fact an army veteran who had lost a leg whilst serving in Iraq.

He had a regular spot right outside the arches which meant at least he could sleep under cover each night after his day's work of playing Scottish sounding music on an out of tune old accordion, well more of a small squeeze box type concertina, whilst sitting on a threadbare old armchair with his Long John Silver type crutch leaning by its side.

Angus and his squeeze box seemed to almost wheeze in harmony whilst collecting bits of small change in a plastic cup on the floor from the occasional kindly passer bye.

Billy had always had a bit of a soft spot for Angus and would sometimes take him a sandwich or a bit of chocolate or something to eat when he was on duty on the railway arches route. Angus would always say the same thing, *"you are a good man PC Oliver."*

He stopped to say a quick *"how are you"*, to which the now almost skeletal framed grey bearded Scotsman just nodded with a wide smile as he always did, showing the few teeth, he still had.

Billy walked on, then suddenly stopped for a second, turned back and gave his fish and chips to old Angus.

Old Angus narrowed his eyes and stared at Billy for a minute as if delving deep into his mind's memory, then finally smiled and said, *"You are a good man PC Oliver".*

When he got home, Billy also began to go over the unsolved case of the murdered photographer. He wanted to see more of the photographic coverage taken at the scene plus the exhibits that were referred to which were found in the room and were preserved.

He also wanted to know more about the studio room layout and the rest of the old 3 storey Georgian terraced building which was apparently not only Mr Dorsey's workplace studio but also his home.

That is the area Billy decided he would be concentrating on when they met up the following day at their *"new HQ".*

CHAPTER 4

When Dan arrived at the office the next morning, Billy was already there. He was sat in his chair twisting it around from side to side.

"Sounds like you've solved your squeaky chair problem then Billy?"

"Yep" replied Billy with a broad smile, spinning a complete squeak free circle.

"Where's the boy wonder then"? said Dan.

"Would you believe he was told he didn't need to come in until this afternoon to allow the brains of the unit, namely us two, to decide on the areas of research we need him to look into" replied Billy.

"What's you're thinking from what we know so far then Sherlock" said Billy".

Dan said he was going to go through all the witness statements again starting with Victer Collier, a young 21-year-old who had been working at the studio for a short period before Arnold Dorsey was murdered.

Billy said he wanted to concentrate on all the known information gathered from the crime scene, what records were found about the victim's client lists and diaries and see if the photographer had any assistants or staff who may have worked for him.

They agreed they needed to see the results of the postmortem again and see if an approximate time of death had been established.

Do we know Mr Dorsey's family history? What happened to the photography business? Did anyone take it over?

It was known that within a couple of years of Dorsey's death, all the adjoining Georgian buildings were bought by a property development company and were converted into one very expensive large standalone luxury apartment block with the grand name of Imperial Court. Just one of the cheaper apartments, even back then would command a purchase price of anything above half a million.

These, along with other questions would be the basis for their young

IT assistant Shivi to carry out his research.

The remainder of the morning went quick, with both Dan and Billy ploughing through the boxed files, each making notes along the way.

"I guess this is working inside the box as opposed to thinking outside the box" said Dan, looking over at Billy.

A gentle knock came on the door. Neither barely looked up from their deep concentration. A second slightly louder knock prompted Billy to shout, *"come in the door's not locked".*

The door opened slowly, and Shivi popped his head around.

Dan looked at his watch and said, *"Blimey, it's 12.45, come in Shivi, you don't have to knock, you work here remember, this is your office as well".*

Shivi came in and took off his coat and shoulder bag, while nodding and politely saying *"Mr Nichols, Mr Oliver".* He took out a small laptop from his bag and sat down at his "workstation" which now resembled a NASA ground base station.

"Look, forget the formalities Shivi, it's Dan and Billy, we will be working together from now on" said Dan, and there's no need to knock on the door."

Shivi sat down at his desk and began to switch on all his technical equipment and as he moved around, his chair started squeaking with every swivel.

Dan looked over at Billy, who half looked up, unable to conceal a smirk. Dan shook his head from side to side and said under his breath *"you rotten sod Billy".*

Shivi was now on his knees underneath his chair trying to figure out where the squeak had suddenly come from.

"We've made a list of some research we'd like you to do Shivi please," said Dan.

"But fix that squeak on your chair first eh, it's annoying" Billy said.

Things seem to settle down after that and all three got down to the serious business in hand.

It turned out that Shivi was very proficient and was producing the research reports well. Dan was impressed, and even Billy finally had to admit their young IT assistant was going to be an asset.

"You know he operates that workstation almost as good as I do my own D J workstation," said Billy.

"Oh, so your D J deck is now a workstation is it?" said Dan.

"Shall I go and get us some coffee? Shivi said, now actually feeling a real part of the team.

"Well, that's very civil of you Shivindra" said Billy. "And remember, there no need to knock on the door when you get back".

Shivi responded be swivelling a complete 360 circle in his chair, demonstrating not a single squeak before jumping up, and all three team members laughed.

"He's a nice young fella," said Billy. *"Yes, he is"* replied Dan with a broad knowing smile.

Dan now looking serious said, *"You know when you said to Shivi earlier that he didn't need to knock, the door is open, it got me thinking, why was the door to Dorsey's place unlocked when the delivery man arrived the morning his body was found?*

His statement said that in the past he had always arrived with deliveries well before the studio was open for business at Mr Dorsey's specific request, and he always had to ring the bell for Dorsey to let him in".

"So, the delivery fella when he gets no response, just tries the main door, finds it open and then finds the second door unlocked as well, and just walks in, shouts "anyone at home" then finds Dorsey brown bread on the studio floor and rings three nine's, said Billy.

"There was no evidence of forced entry in any other part of the building, so Dorsey himself must have let the murderer in and therefore may have already known him", continued Billy.

"Well for someone who could attack him so savagely and cause such horrific injuries, particularly to his head and face suggests to me he not only knew the person, and we are assuming it was a male at this point, but he must have had a personal reason for attacking Dorsey in that way, and we have to wonder what that reason could have been", Dan said.

Shivi arrived back with the refreshments and looked more comfortable than ever. He was smiling and said a young female at the coffee machine had smiled at him.

"I hope you smiled back", said Billy *"you must point her out to me next time".*

Shivi was back in his now squeak free chair and Dan said,

"Can you do a full family tree on our victim Mr Dorsey please Shivi, I mean a full tree, upwards downwards and sideways, let's get to know a bit more about our victim's background".

"No probs boss" replied Shivi, now feeling confident.

Billy added, *"and do a full search on the victim's photography business, any reported high-profile clients, any reports in the press where Dorsey's photographs were used, any adverse publicity as well as good, and anything on social media".*

"Can do boss" replied Shivi, now feeling ten foot tall.

The photographs and a topography plan of the victim's address showed that the old 3 storey Georgian terraced building was roughly the middle property of the row and situated in what was at the time the houses were built, considered to be an area of affluence.

The building immediately to the right side of the studio at the time of the murder was let off as offices, the one on the left was divided as six small flats as were most of the remaining terrace, many of which were pretty run down and in need of some care and attention.

The main entrance to Dorsey's studio facing the street was via a front door which led to a tiny porch, then a second inner door giving access to the main building. Both the outer and inner doors were always kept locked at night requiring two separate individual keys.

The immediate entrance space had been used as a small reception area situated just to the left of the staircase which led to the upper rooms and the photographers private living quarters.

A further downstairs door led into the studio itself, which had been set out with a variety of ceiling mounted spotlights, different types of cameras on tripods, a raised platform in one corner with a couple of chairs and different backdrops presumably for formal group photographs etc.

Billy had the box of most of the items that had been taken from the scene, documented and stored, and had been looking through them.

He found some items from the photographer's desk plus what appeared to be an appointment diary, also a couple of framed photographs which looked like they could be Mr Dorsey's family members. Also, a small bunch of 3 keys, 2 of which fitted the 2 front entrance doors, the 3rd a smaller key which did not seem to fit the desk drawers or any other storage cabinets in which the photographic equipment was kept.

Further searches later discovered the key was to a safe, which was found in one of Dorsey's private rooms upstairs. The safe contained some paperwork plus cash totalling just short of £9,000 in used notes. There was no obvious explanation or reason why Dorsey should have that kind of cash. His formal business accounts had been scrutinised and all were in order with formal invoices accounted for with his clients.

Why would he be holding so much cash and where did it come from.

Plenty to think about and bounce off each other Billy thought.

All in all, it hadn't been a bad day, and the two old pals decided it would be a good idea to call in at the Crown and Anchor again for a quick debrief, maybe helped along with a beer.

CHAPTER 5

Now back at old HQ, at their almost permanent corner table, or "workstation 2" as Billy had started to call it, with a welcome beer they chinked glasses and said cheers, after what they both thought had been quite a satisfying first real day.

"He's OK Shivi, I knew he would fit in," Billy said. *"Yep, I could see it right from the start Danny boy".*

Dan just rolled his eyes and took another sip of his beer.

Billy continued, *"you know when Shivi mentioned a young woman had smiled at him at the station today? well it reminded me, I meant to mention to you, do you remember a lad called Peter Knight who was in our year at school, not in our class, but the same year".*

"No, I don't remember him" replied Dan".

"He wasn't from our estate, he lived in one of the streets off Waterloo Road in a terraced house", Billy went on.

"No, I don't remember him," said Dan.

"You do, he walked with a bit of a run", persisted Billy.

"Walked with a bit of a run? are you having me on Billy? how do you mean?".

"Like a bit of a half skip, it was sort of like one leg was in a rush, and the other was just strolling and couldn't quite catch up, you remember, he was a bit of a smart arse, a right big head" continued Billy.

"No Billy, I don't remember him, anyway, what about him?

"Well, he had a sister, about three or four years young than him".

"Get to the point Billy before one of us dies please."

"Well, she was called Evelyn, but they called her Eve", Billy went on.

"Please Billy, the suspense is killing me," said Dan.

"Well, Eve worked at the Police Station as a typist when I was there, I've not seen her for years, but I remember she was really nice, and quite a good looker".

"And?" said Dan.

"Well, I just wondered if she still works at the Station. I remember she lost her husband quite a few years back".

"Is there a point to all this then Billy?" said Dan, now looking into his empty glass.

"OK, I get the message Danny boy, you are not interested, and you want a fill up" said Billy getting up to go to the bar, then turned around said," *I can't believe you don't remember Peter Knight".*

Back with the beers Billy went on, *"Peter Knight, you know, each time we heard anyone at school say his name, we both used to say, "before you go to bed".*

"What you on about Billy?

"Peter Knight, pee tonight before you go to bed".

"I sometimes worry about you Billy, have you ever considered standing for the Raving Loony Party"?

CHAPTER 6

Some of Mr Dorsey's online background research uncovered by Shivi found that he had inherited the photography business from his father Charles Dorsey who had passed away when Arnold was aged 25.

Arnold Dorsey had worked in his father's business after completing his college education studying art, and later photography. He had never married and lived alone in the large 3-storey building which he had also inherited as an only child.

Mr Dorsey had employed a young chap as his assistant in the studio, and to occasionally look after the small reception desk in the entrance.

According to his statement, Victor Collier was aged 21 and had apparently met Mr Dorsey at an Art and Greek Mythology evening class in the town centre where they shared common interests.

From all accounts Victor Collier was a quiet shy young man who appeared to gain some confidence from working for Mr Dorsey.

Dan had briefly read through his Police statement but needed to read through it again.

"This young assistant, Victor Collier, in his statement said that he had only worked at the studio for a few months then left. It was shortly afterwards that Dorsey was found murdered. He didn't say why he had left after such a short period other than saying that he didn't feel the job suited him, he didn't elaborate.

The statement is void of any real detail when you look at it, basically, yes and no answers", continued Dan.

"Well Sherlock, let's get our boy wonder here in mission control to update his details and we will go and pay him a polite visit," said Billy.

"Some more research Shivi, we need to confirm the address of one of the witnesses Victor Collier, see if he is still at the same address as on his statement and if not, we need his present address.

And find out which company redeveloped the properties and converted them into Imperial Court, we need that".

"On it boss," Shivi was enjoying this.

Arnold Dorsey's diary listed the names of his business clients, their appointment dates and venues etc. and threw up a few surprises when Billy had gone through it.

"Look at this Danny boy", showing Dan the diary.

"Quite a substantial business by the looks of it", Dan said turning the pages, which revealed some names who would have been considered high-profile people in the community at the time, local businessmen, Council officers and even the Lord Mayor's office.

It appeared that Mr Dorsey was very well connected and was regularly called upon to cover many formal events.

"I've got the latest recorded address for Victor Collier, it's the same as on his Police statement. I have included the name of the female listed there as well", said Shivi.

"Good thinking Shivi, well done, that's tickety boo", said Billy winking over to Dan.

"What are you going to do now then"? Shivi asked.

"You will find that most crimes are solved with the help of real people, the public, not just computers young man", answered Billy.

"Who said, the Police are the public and the public are the Police Shivi?", Billy continued.

"What?" said Shivi looking up from his chair.

"Who said, the Police are the public and the public are the Police"? repeated Billy.

Shivi looked a bit puzzled and eventually said *"You just did"*.

Billy rolled his eyes. *"Didn't they teach you anything other than how to be an IT wizard at Police College"?* he said.

"Well, to be fair Billy, technically Shivi's answer was correct, you did just say that" said Dan with a wide smile.

"Oh, very good, thank you Sherlock, I'm trying educate boy wonder here," Billy snapped.

"Sir Robert Peel", said Billy, *"look him up Shivi, the founder of the modern-day Police Force, born not many miles from where you are sitting right now, in Bury". "I didn't know that"* replied Shivi.

"Well here endeth today's lesson" said Billy, in a noticeably softer tone, clearly realising he must have sounded a bit harsh on Shivi.

After a short silence and Billy feeling a little bit sorry, he went over to Shivi's chair and said, *"Can you print off the address stuff for Collier?"* giving Shivi a half pat on the shoulder, shielding the gesture a bit with his body, hoping Dan didn't see it.

He's a big softy really, thought Dan smiling to himself.

Dan probably knew his old pal Billy better than any other person.

CHAPTER 7

Before setting off to the address shown for Collier Dan had a look at Shivi's print out.

"Look at this Billy, there is also a Rose Collier listed living with Victor Collier at his address, there was no mention of a Mrs Collier in his original statement," said Dan.

"Well, that was around 10 years ago, what if he got married, he will be in his early 30's now" Billy replied.

"Let's see if Collier himself can enlighten us then eh Billy?" said Dan looking at Shivi's printout again, *Collier's address is not too far".*

The semi-detached house was just on the outskirts of the city. The exterior of the property appeared quite drab and old fashioned.

There was no bell, so Billy knocked heavily on the door in his usual manner, perfected in his PC days.

After a while, with no response at all, the two were just about to walk away with Billy saying, *"I had a feeling it would be one of those days",* when the door opened.

Before either man could speak, they were greeted with an abrupt, *"What do you want, who are you?"*

The lady who stood in front of them appeared to be aged in her mid to late 50's and was dressed in a dark well-worn dress over which she had tied around her waist an old-fashioned apron, her greying hair brushed back from her pale face.

"Sorry to disturb you madam", we would like a word with Victor if it's convenient, we are from the Police," said Billy showing his ID.

"He's not here, what do you want him for?" came the sharp reply.

"Any idea what time he will be home?" Dan asked.

"He won't be, he doesn't live here" she snapped.

"Do you know where we can find him then madam?" Dan continued.

"No, I don't" she replied, starting to close the door.

Billy, now losing what little patience he had said, *"Look madam, this is official, we need to speak to Victor Collier, and you are not being very helpful, in fact you are being obstructive, perhaps we should talk back at the Police station. Your name please?* As he reached for his notebook.

She paused and said, *"I am Victor's mother, Rose Collier, I think you should come in then"* realising Billy was having none of her aggressive attitude.

Over the next hour, the two cold case men listened intently to the unexpected and surprising account of what the lady had to tell them.

On the drive back to the office Dan and Billy went over the day's events and tried to make sense of what their enquiries had found.

"Shivi, I want you to sit in on this," said Billy.

"We arrived at Victor Collier's address and the first surprise of the day, was to discover that Rose Collier turns out to be Victor's mother, not his wife as we first speculated.

After some reluctance she told us that her son Victor left home within a few months of Mr Dorsey's murder and she has not seen nor heard from him since, not in all these years, and has no idea where he is, that was the second surprise", explained Billy.

Shivi said, *"Can I ask a question, do we know if Victor had an alibi for the time of the murder, and I wonder if he attended Dorsey's funeral."That's a good question" said Dan, "let's check through the statements again, but I doubt if there any way of checking who was at the funeral after 10 years".*

"And now the only person who will know if he was at the funeral has gone AWOL", said Billy.

"I'm sure Collier had a rock-solid alibi" as Dan shuffled through his folders. *"Yep, here it is, he was with a friend, a Miss Krystna Bartosz and she confirmed it".*

"Well let's see if you can work your IT magic Shivi and come up with a clue as to exactly where we can find Mr Victor Collier, as we need to have a more intimate chat", Billy continued.

"I think we should speak to his mother again Billy, she was reluctant to talk in the first place, and even then, I got the distinct impression she wasn't

being completely open, surely she should know if he attended the funeral, she may have been there herself".

"That's a good idea Dan, but let's have some coffee before we burst into action again eh Shivi? who knows you may bump into that young lady by the coffee machine again, and if you do, take a tip from one who knows, and ask her name", Billy said with a wink.

While they were alone Billy said, *"You remember me mentioning Peter Knight the other day Dan?".*

"Please, don't start all that again Billy, we've got work to do".

"No no, I asked around in the station, and his sister Eve does still work as a civilian here".

"I'm very pleased for you Billy, what is your point?" replied Dan, still looking through his notes.

"Well, you know, I just thought, well you know," said Billy.

"You know what Billy"?

"I just thought we may ask her out for a drink with us, you know Dan".

"You mean ask her out for a drink with you Billy", Dan said still not looking up from his paperwork.

"No, keep your deerstalker on Sherlock, I will be working my magic from my DJ workstation a week on Friday, remember it's the first Friday of the month at the Golden Ball and I'm hoping to meet up with Jenny and I thought it may be nice if you came along, and we could see if Eve is free".

"I don't even know this Eve, I've never met her before and how do you know she didn't remarry, or be in a steady relationship"?

Leave those details to me Danny boy, you just make sure you've got a clean shirt ironed on that Friday night", said Billy with a wink.

Shivi came back with the drinks wearing a broad smile, *"She's called Miranda, I spoke to her, and I think she might like me".*

"Stick with us kid, and you won't go wrong", Billy said patting their IT assistant on the back.

CHAPTER 8

DI Mike Morris wanted a meeting in his new office, which was in a small but new modern wing of the station.

"It's about time they updated some of this building" Billy said as the two made their way across the ground floor of the station and then up a short flight of stairs to a sort of mezzanine floor where Mike's new office was now situated.

On one side of the corridor leading to the office was a quite large open plan office which housed the various admin staff members. The entire working space was visible through the large glass panels which stretched the full length of the corridor.

"Hang on a minute Dan, I think I can see Eve, the lady I was telling you about, look, over in that far corner, the one with the short blonde hair and neat figure", said Billy.

Just then the door at the end of the corridor opened and Mike Morris said, *"come on in lads"*.

"Very nice" said Billy looking around the small office and in particular Mike's smart modern desk and padded swivel chair.

"Take a seat and fill me in where we are up to on this photographer case" Mike said pointing to the two smart chairs facing him.

After going through what had been established so far, and more importantly what had not been established, DI Morris explained that "the powers that be" had decided they would announce in the media that the unsolved murder of Mr Dorsey was being looked at again by a new cold case review team, and appeal for anyone with any information, however small should call in, even anonymously, on a dedicated number. All information received would be passed to their office and collated by Shivendra.

"Well, we had better go and inform boy wonder that he will have the pleasure of dealing with incoming information from all the fruits and nuts in Manchester, with all sorts of weird and wonderful claims that they know who the murderer is. I bet one will be that he was killed by an alien

from *Mars or an Elvis lookalike who killed him with a Fender guitar while singing All Shook Up,"* Billy said.

On the way back down the corridor Billy was trying to see if he could pick out Eve again, but he couldn't. *"I'll just pop inside to see if it was Eve"*, he said.

"I'll see you back downstairs at the office then" Dan replied, feeling uncomfortable at even the thought of going into the large office unannounced and not knowing a single person in the room, and the vast majority of who were females.

That thought of course never even entered Billy's mind.

Back at their office Dan found Shivi printing out some stuff.

"Any joy with locating Victor Collier's present whereabouts Shivi?"

"Not a sausage Dan, I've done credit searches from his last known address and a general name sweep on his name, which is not really a common name, it's like he has disappeared of the face of the earth".

"What if he died", said Dan.

"Nope" replied Shivi, *"I have checked for deaths".*

Neither had noticed Billy had just arrived back in the room. "What if he could have gone abroad", Billy chipped in, hearing their conversation.

"Or what if he changed his name", said Shivi, *"Did you know that another man with the same name as Mr Dorsey changed his name to the singer Englebert Humperdink"*, he continued.

"How did you know that?" said Dan looking surprised.

"Last night's music quiz in my local pub" replied Shivi.

"I didn't know you were into music" Billy said, *"I'm a seasoned DJ myself and a bit of a font of knowledge on music and singers"*, he went on, trying to sound in a matter-of-fact casual way whilst shuffling the folders on his desk.

"Oh yes, I love the weekly quiz nights, especially the music questions" Shivi replied.

"How come you didn't know Englebert's real name was Arnold Dorsey then Billy, I mean you being a music, Guru?" Dan said, trying to sound serious

and winking over at Shivi.

"I did know that Dan, everyone knows that it's common knowledge" Billy replied trying not to make eye contact with the other two.

After a short silence Dan took a sneaky sideways glance towards Shivi and very quietly started singing "please release me set me free". Shivi got the hint and joined in.

Billy looked up and said, *"All right, all right, I get the message".*

Then realising he was beaten for today said, *"We should explain the Boss's plan to go public on the case review Dan".*

Over the remainder of the day, Billy laid out what was likely to happen once a media appeal had been made for information about the murder, and that calls to the dedicated number would be relayed to their office. Their little review case team would have their work cut out for sure.

CHAPTER 9

"You know when we were having our favourite "what if" session the other day" Dan said, "well we shouldn't totally dismiss the point that Shivi made, what if Victor Collier did change his name for some reason"?

"Fair point Danny boy, a person can quite legally change their name by Deed Poll and there is no register you can search to check that. I know certain conditions apply, such as if a person for instance has a conviction for a sex offence etc., we'll get Shivi to look up the full legal conditions that must be complied with, just in case".

"I was also thinking earlier, who identified Dorsey's body Billy?

I'm pretty sure it was Victor Collier Dan, but I thought it would be worth speaking to the pathologist who carried out the autopsy anyway".

The pathologist was recorded as Dr Derek Armstrong, a well-known and respected specialist in his field and DI Morris had arranged for Dan and Billy to pay him a visit.

Back in the office the phone rang, Shivi answered, *"Review team office, can I help"*. The voice said, *"Major Tom to ground control"*.

"Who is this?" Shivi replied thinking it was probably one of the fruits and nuts Billy had told him to expect from a member of the public with information about the case.

"It's me, Billy, you turnip, I want you to research the legalities that must apply if someone wants to change their name by Deed Poll".

"Will do, Billy, changing your name to Major Tom then?"

"That's actually quite funny coming from you Shivi, now get on with it, we are on our way to see the Pathologist who carried out the postmortem", Billy replied.

"You know I am actually warming to our IT assistant Dan" he continued with a chuckle as the two made their way to Oldham.

Mike Morris had described Dr Derek Armstrong as a jovial character considering the nature of his work and said he was sure his forensic examination on Mr Dorsey's savaged body would have been very thorough.

They arrived at Royal Oldham Hospital and were directed to Dr Armstrong's office where they were welcomed by the rather overweight, ruddy faced Doctor who greeted them with a wide smile and a firm handshake.

Dan couldn't help thinking that he had just shaken a hand that had probably spent most of its working time inside some poor sod's opened up body, and it gave him a little shiver.

"I know it was around ten years ago, but I recall the case quite well gentlemen" he said as he opened the bulky folder on his desk.

Showing no emotion and continuing his broad smile the Pathologist went through his notes and confirmed his findings that the cause of death was strangulation by hands, and very strong hands gentlemen he added. The victim's Laryngeal Prominence, the Adam's Apple in layman's terms, had been heavily and continuously depressed, depriving the body of air, and death would have been swift.

The mutilation of the face appeared to have been caused immediately after death. The right eyeball was hanging out of its socket and the remainder of the face, particularly around the mouth had been beaten. A front tooth had been knocked out during the facial assault adding to the blood spillage seeping from the mouth.

There was no evidence that any other part of the body had been attacked or beaten, with one exception the victim's testicles and immediate upper surrounding inner leg areas were badly bruised.

Time of death was estimated between 6 to 10 hours prior to the body being discovered. Mr Dorsey was fully dressed indicating he was up and about on that morning or was killed late on the previous evening he concluded.

All this conveyed via the Pathologist's eloquent old-school well-educated accent.

"Any questions gentlemen?" asked the still smiling Dr Armstrong.

Both Dan and Billy responded eagerly, both immediately saying *"Yes"*.

"Well one at a time eh", came the response, as the friendly expert

seemed to be enjoying his own work being discussed.

"When you say that strangulation was by very strong hands Doctor, are you suggesting that the assailant was a male?" Billy said. "And would there have been any fingerprints on the neck?".

"There were no fingerprints or DNA on any part of the victim, and the only blood sample analysis were shown to be that of Mr Dorsey himself.

I should add that my role does not include suggesting the murderer was male or female, simply that my findings were that it would have taken considerable strength to hold down and strangle the victim".

Dan asked, *"Do you remember the person who came and identified the body"?*

"Yes, I do", Dr Armstrong said looking again at his notes, *"I remember quite well, Mr Victor Collier was a slightly built young man who was extremely nervous, and I was surprised that he was having to carry out what is after all not the most pleasant of tasks alone, presumably as there was no relative of the victim available."*

"Do you have any other questions gentlemen" he continued looking at his watch, *"it's strange that I seem to be more popular with people when they are dead",* he said", still smiling, *"If you do have any further questions, please just give me a call, and please just call me Derek"* he said handing Billy a card with his direct number on.

"Just one more question doctor, I mean Derek," said Billy.

"So, our victim was purposely left with a face like Quasimodo, and just for good luck was given a kick in the orchestra stalls. To me that suggests the attacker was a man, or if not, it had to be a 20 stone female rugby player, is that about right?"

"Well, I suppose one could look at it that way, but that must be for you gentlemen to establish in your search for the person who carried out the brutal attack", the friendly Pathologist replied.

He stood and offered out a hand of farewell to Billy and then to Dan, who accepted, but still with that uncomfortable feeling as he looked down at his own open hand hoping the Pathologist hadn't noticed.

Just as they were leaving the room the still smiling doctor said to Billy,

"For what it is worth, I tend to agree with your hypothesis, but I wouldn't have quite put it in the vernacular way that you did".

On the drive back both men were clearly deep in thought at what they had heard, and there was little conversation for a while.

"By the time we get back into Manchester the office will be closed for the day Dan, shall we head back and have a debrief at the Crown and Anchor?"

Before Dan had time to answer, Billy's mobile rang.

"Ground control to Major Tom", Shivi's unmistakeable voice came through. Billy put it on loudspeaker. *"What is it boy wonder?".*

"Couple of things, re Victor Collier, I have been researching social media sites and found that he was active a while back on a couple of forums but that ceased some time ago, I thought if I can make a note of the people he used to share with, maybe that could give us a lead?

"That's really good thinking Shivi" shouted Dan from the driver's seat.

"Good idea" added Billy, *"and if you look in the file on my desk, you will see Dorsey's diary showing names of his clients with venue and booking dates etc. I know it's going back ten years but compile a list of those people and their current addresses etc., we need to start broadening our enquiries. See you in the office in the morning".*

"Oh, just one more thing" said Shivi, *I think we may have started to see some calls from the media appeal coming in. An officer from the front desk popped in earlier, he said a fella who he described as a tramp came into the Station with a bit of folded paper with writing on it which said "for PC Oliver. The Police Station, Letsby Avenue".*

Initially the Desk Officer said there wasn't a PC Oliver working at this station, but one of the older officers suggested it could be you Billy ".

"What did the note say Shivi?"

"I've got it here, it just had scribbled on it, Angus"

"And nothing else?"

"No, nothing, just the name Angus" replied Shivi.

"OK, see you tomorrow" said Billy ending the call and now frowning a bit.

"What's all that about then Billy?"

"I don't really know Danny boy, but we can talk about it when we get to the pub eh Sherlock, I am ready for a drink".

CHAPTER 10

"*Cheers Dan, I was ready for this"* Billy said as they settled in their corner and clinked their beer glasses.

"What did you think about our jolly Pathologist's findings, apparently Dorsey wasn't a small fella, so the person who attacked him must have been pretty powerful to hold him down and strangle him with his bare hands, it had to be a man surely".

"Obviously not with his bare hands though Billy, the examination showed no traces of DNA on Dorsey's clothes or skin, so our Mr X must have been wearing gloves and obviously came prepared" Dan pointed out.

"Anyway, what's all this Angus business about Billy?"

Billy then proceeded to tell his story of old Angus from his PC days, leaving Dan with a mental picture of the old Scotsman playing his accordion by the railway arch.

After listening intently, clinging on to every word Dan paused for a minute, narrowed his eyes and said, *"Hang on, hang on Billy, are you winding me up?"*

"What do you mean winding you up?" Billy said as he got up to get more drinks.

"You're telling me, you know an old Scottish army veteran who can play a squeeze box with one leg", Dan said.

"No, you turnip, weren't you listening? he doesn't play the thing with his leg", Billy said raising his eyes and tutting all the way to the bar.

"I never know when you are being serious or not" replied Dan.

Back with the drinks Billy said, *"Dan honestly, I'm dead serious about old Angus, everything I have told you is absolutely true; I swear on my mother's gravy"*, Dan laughed even though he had heard Billy's joke before.

"Anyway, didn't Shivi say the bit of paper was addressed to PC Oliver at the Police Station on Letsby Avenue, what does that mean?"

"Well, when Angus used to ask me where I lived, I would always joke and say, the Station on Letsby Avenue, just a joke Danny boy, you know, ***Let's***

***be having you*"*.*

Both men laughed and raised their glasses, but Dan could tell this Angus message was troubling his old pal.

Changing the subject Dan said, *"Just thinking about Collier, I know he had a rock-solid alibi and just doesn't fit with anything we heard today, but I just get the feeling he knew more than he said at the time.*

It sounds to me like he was scared, even scared enough to leave home and disappear off the radar shortly after the murder, and I wonder what would make him do that?".

"I tend to agree with your hypothesis, but not necessarily put in the vernacular way you put it" Billy said smiling and trying to mimic Dr Armstrong's posh voice.

"That's very funny Billy, but I'm trying to be serious here".

"Lighten up Sherlock, why don't **you** *do something funny now, like go and get the drinks in"*, Billy said, as he waived his empty glass.

CHAPTER 11

Back home that night, Dan started to make a list of what they could do to move their investigation forward.

He thought they should have another word with Collier's mother Rose as he felt something just wasn't quite right and she wasn't being completely open. She must know more than she was saying.

They hadn't had Shivi's research report on which development company now owns Dorsey's old house/studio building, as apparently, he had no surviving relatives who may have inherited, and was it never investigated whether he made a will. He was adding all these to his growing list.

Going over their meeting that day with Dr Armstrong, Dan couldn't help trying to visualise the image of the way Dorsey's body had been found, the disfigurement of the face and the kicking between the legs, surely intended as a revenge punishment.

He wondered about the eye hanging out on a thread and the tooth being knocked out.

He suddenly thought more about the tooth. The Dr said it had been knocked out after strangulation, but his report didn't mention the tooth again. It couldn't have been swallowed after death surely? was it found at the scene? If so, it would have been preserved and stored with other items the Scene of Crimes team would have gathered.

We must look through the photographs again he thought and added that to his list.

It was really time he turned in for the night, it had been a long day but the more he thought about the tooth, the more it played on his mind. What if it wasn't found at the scene and it hadn't been swallowed, where was it?

If the body had been purposely left in such a horrible state, face looking like Quasimodo and kicked in the orchestra stalls as Billy had so succinctly put it, then the message clearly wasn't just for Dorsey himself as he was already dead. Then who else could this visual message have been intended for?

He couldn't stop thinking about the eye and the tooth. An eye for an eye, a tooth for a tooth, he couldn't get this out of his head, and finally nodded off trying to remember where the saying was from.

.... O ....

Shivi was already hard at work when Dan arrived the next morning and it was clear that he was enjoying his role.

"Did you manage to get the current ownership details of Dorsey's old address Shivi?"

"Yep, it's here Dan, it was apparently unsold for quite a while before the whole row was eventually bought by a development company, all the details are in this folder. The company is called Focus Properties. Focus eh, If Dorsey is up there looking down, he may be pleased with that name, eh? Shivi said.

"Or even down there looking up eh" Dan said.

He had borrowed heavily on the property to the extent that the banks and a building society had several legal charges on his building and basically, they owned the property, he had virtually no equity in it.

Just then Billy arrived. *"Good morning campers how are we all today?"*.

Both Dan and Shivi were now deep into what they were doing and neither even looked up and just mumbled quietly "good morning".

"Well, good morning, how are you Billy, how nice to see you on this bright and sunny morning", Billy sarcastically said out loud before hanging his coat up on the back of the door and settling behind his desk.

"I've been thinking Billy", Dan said, still looking down at his notes and ever-growing paperwork.

"Oh, I didn't realise you were there Dan", Billy said. *How are you this morning?"*

"I think we should have another word with Rose Collier. Did she give a statement to the Police at the time?" Dan asked.

Before Billy had time to answer Shivi said, *"No, I don't see one here Dan".*

"And have we got the folder with the Scene of Crime photographs?" Dan went on.

"Shall I answer? I am here you know" Billy said reaching in his desk draw for the photograph folder. *"Looking for something in particular Sherlock are you?".*

"Dr Armstrong explained that Dorsey had a tooth knocked out by his attacker, can you remember seeing the discarded tooth anywhere on any of the photos?". Dan said.

"Can't say that I did to be honest", Billy replied, "let's go through them again".

After going through every single shot, they could see no trace of a tooth.

"What if he swallowed it, or it was lodged in the back of his throat?" Billy suggested.

"Tell you what Dan, why don't you ring the Pathologist, he should be able to clear it up, here's his card, I'm going to pay old Angus a visit to find out what this message is all about. We can catch up later".

Shivi chipped in, *"Just before you go, I meant to ask Billy, what is Angus surname? just so we have a record on file".*

"Funny, none of us ever knew his second name, he was never in any trouble where he had to have his collar felt, so there was no need to ask, we just used to call him Angus McCoatup", Billy said as he unhooked his own coat from the door and left, but not before turning round with a cheeky wink.

CHAPTER 12

Dan's first call to Dr Armstrong went through to his voicemail so he assumed the Pathologist must be in theatre probably carrying out a postmortem. Just the thought of that made Dan shudder as he visualised "Derek" with sleeves rolled up and long rubber gloves covered in blood rummaging around inside some poor sod's internal organs.

He suggested Shivi go to get them some coffee while he tried to clear his mind and concentrate on the other issues.

While things were quiet, Dan's thoughts wandered back again to the saying, "an eye for and, a tooth for a tooth" which was still really bugging him, where had he heard it?

Right out of the blue, he remembered a couple of nights previously he had his TV on, not watching, just in the background.

It was all about ancient aliens and was set in Egypt. The various ancient stone carvings depicted strange beings coming down from the skies who were thought of as Gods, there were endless examples, some images appeared to have sort of space helmets on, all very strange. The theory was that we were visited by these beings from other galaxies thousands of years ago.

Then it was quoting passages from the Old Testament and how Moses was guided by God leading the Israelites out of Egypt to the promised land and the narrative included the words "an eye for an eye, a tooth for a tooth.

"That's it," he said out loud, it had to be, it makes sense, reciprocal retribution. The punishment to mirror the crime.

An eye for an eye, a tooth for a tooth, it's a biblical phrase.

It **was** a message, but not just for Dorsey, but some other person as well. Who could that be, a religious man? and what had Dorsey done to deserve such a punishment?

Shivi came back with the coffee and said, *"Have you managed to get through to the pathologist yet Dan?"*

Dan snapped out of his deep thought and said, *"Just going to try him again now".*

This time the friendly Pathologist answered.

"Sorry to trouble you Doctor, but you did say if we had any further questions, we could give you a call.

"No problem, stay on the line while I just finished scrubbing up" he replied in his cheery voice.

I wish he hadn't said that Dan thought as he now had visions of blood being swilled down a plug hole and the happy Dr wiping his hands dry.

"Now then Officer, what can I do for you?"

Dan reminded the Dr about the tooth which according to his report had been knocked out during the vicious pounding of the victim face and asked if the missing tooth had definitely been knocked out during the attack and couldn't have been a very recent extraction by Dorsey's dentist?

The Dr laughed and said there was no doubt whatsoever that the tooth had been loosened by the heavy blows to the face, particularly to the mouth area. In fact, he added, that he thought the tooth had possibly been finally removed by hand after the initial blows, as the gum area all around the tooth base had been stretched all the way around as if by loosening.

Dan thought, well I don't remember him telling us that the other day.

Dan went on to explain that they couldn't see the presence of the removed tooth anywhere on the scene of crime photographs and wondered if it could had been stuffed down the victim's throat, and Dorsey could have ingested it?

The latter was not the case the Dr explained, as there had been a full toxicology examination of the internal organs and there was no tooth present.

"What if the tooth had become lodged in the victim's clothing?" asked Dan.

"We can rule that out also, as all outer and inner clothing had been thoroughly examined, all pockets searched, and contents logged" replied Dr Armstrong.

"So, the missing tooth was never found at the scene? is that correct?"

"That is correct officer",

"Well thank you for your valuable time, Doctor" Dan replied.

Dan couldn't wait to tell Billy when his mobile rang.

"Where are you Billy? I need to speak to you urgently, I've got things to tell you".

"Calm down Danny boy, I've just left Angus and, on my way, back. See you at the C n A in half an hour, I've got things to tell you as well Sherlock".

Now sat in the Crown & Anchor Dan said *"You go first Billy"* as the two had their first sip of beer.

"OK, I get to the railway arches and there's no sign of old Angus sat in his usual spot outside, I go inside the archways and spot him sat in a corner on his old armchair alongside what is obviously his sleeping area consisting of a mattress on the floor, well a mattress sized off-cut piece of yellow foam rubber covered by a few old blankets.

It really is a crime Dan that someone who fought for his country and loses a limb in action should end up living like this.

Anyway, I showed Angus the bit of paper that someone had brought into the station and asked him what was this about".

"Poor fella could hardly breath let alone speak, he was wheezing and pointed over to one of the other three homeless archway residents who clearly had claimed their own permanent plots, like Angus's.

I waived the chap over. He was a big fella with jet black wavey hair and really dark eyes, a bit scary looking if I'm being honest as he lurched over towards me. I can't imagine anyone trying to nick anything from him.

I showed him the piece of paper, and he said in a foreign accent that it was him who took it to the Police station for Angus.

He told me that Angus had his concertina snatched out of his hands last week by a young man, who also stole the few pounds Angus had in his cup. He went on to say that Angus would always pool his money with the rest of them and it helped to buy some food and drink for all four of them to share.

Angus just sat nodding during the conversation and simply said *"you are a good man PC Oliver.*

I gave the big foreign fella a fiver and told him to go and get some food and drink.

I asked Angus what his helpful pal was called, and he managed to wheeze, his name is Polish Joe.

"What are you going to do then Billy?" Dan asked.

"Well, I'll tell you what I'm going to do Danny boy, I'm going to find Angus's squeezebox, which will have been sold for a few quid at a bent second-hand shop, then find the bastard who nicked it, get the money back from the scum bag, and teach him a lesson" replied Billy.

"Hang on, how exactly are you going to do that Billy? don't be daft.

"The ways and means act Danny boy, the ways and means act", said Billy tapping the side of his nose, *"nothing for you to worry about".*

"I thought the message from Angus had something to do with the Dorsey cold case announcement to the media" Dan said.

"To be honest Dan, so did I, until I found out from the boss that the media announcement will not go public until this weekend, and I confirmed that our names will not be made public as being a part of the review team".

"Come on then Sherlock, what have you deduced today then that is so important?" Billy said calming down a bit.

"Don't know where to start really" Dan said. *"Have you heard the saying, an eye for an eye, a tooth for a tooth?"*

"Yeh, it something from Shakespeare, isn't it?" replied Billy.

"No, it's apparently a biblical phrase from the Old Testament in which the words are said to have been given by God to Moses as he led the Israelite's out of Egypt to the promised land, and that the Gods were believed to have been extra-terrestrials".

Billy stopped him in mid flow and said, *"All very interesting Danny boy, but I have a feeling your sermon is going to take a while, so I must go to the waterloo first, or to quote Shakespeare, to pee of not to pee, that is the question".*

Now back settled down Billy said, *"Now what's all this biblical stuff Dan, you're not going all religious, are you?"*

"No Billy, it's just this tele programme the other night, it made me think, it even claimed they believe that aliens were not only visiting planet earth all those thousands of years ago, but they are already here, living amongst us now".

"I can well believe that Dan, I think one of them works behind the bar at The Bull round the corner from the Police Station" said Billy as he took another swig of his beer.

"Do you know, that has puzzled me Billy, talking about The Bull, why do you never go in there?"

"Ah, The Bull Shit Danny boy, as I like to call it, I'll tell you why Dan, because it's full of coppers. Half the station goes in there. I used to do when I first joined, but soon found out it's full of bull shitters.

I remember one ex CID fella, I can't remember his name, always trying to impress anyone who would listen to him, especially the new recruits and the females, telling tales of the big arrests he had made in his long service, in the hope that his audience were daft enough to keep buying him drinks.

He would inevitably get chucked out at closing time and the truth was that he was pensioned off as he couldn't keep off the booze when on duty. A true bullshitter Dan, and he wasn't the only one by a long way.

I don't think I ever saw him buy a drink; I think his favourite song must have been, Don't get Around much Anymore".

Anyway, what's all this eye for an eye Moses stuff?"

Dan then relayed his telephone conversation with Dr Armstrong, stressing that Dorsey's tooth had likely been finally loosened and removed by hand, and that there was no sign of the tooth either on or in Dorsey, or at the scene.

"So, what's your thinking Dan?".

"Reciprocal retribution Billy, you know, the punishment to mirror the crime, "By your deeds, you shall be done" The murderer was seeking revenge for what Dorsey had done, and as proof he has kept the tooth maybe to make the point, an eye for an eye a tooth for a tooth".

"Then what about the eye then Dan, why didn't the murderer take the eye

as well?"

"I imagine that would have been a bit more difficult don't you think Billy? he certainly made sure it was hanging out on a thread for all to see, but who knows, it's not exactly the kind of thing you can slip in your pocket like a tooth is it?"

CHAPTER 13

"Let's have a look at Dorsey's list of clients Shivi, did you do the research of who they were and if they are still around, some of them will have been spoken to at the time, and if so, we should have copies of their statements", Billy said.

"It's all here, there's quite a list" Shivi replied as he handed the hefty folder to Billy.

"Dan said, *"there's no point in both of us going through that lot Billy, I'd like to have another go at Rose Collier, I'm sure she knows more than she is saying, and she should at least know if Victor attended Dorsey's funeral, and she may have even been there herself. What do you think?"*

"Good idea Danny boy, and good luck with that woman, you'll need it".

Dan arrived at Rose Collier's house and was a little surprised by her reaction when she realised Dan was alone, and not accompanied by his more forceful formal partner.

"It's Mr Nichols if you remember Mrs Collier, Dan said, then politely asked if he could ask just a couple more questions. She certainly seemed much more at ease, and after a short hesitation asked him inside.

Mrs Collier readily confirmed that her son Victor had attended Dorsey's funeral, but when asked if she had also attended, her answer surprised Dan by saying, why would I want to go to his funeral, I couldn't stand the man, or his father.

Dan asked if she knew who else was at the funeral.

She said probably his cronies from the Town Hall and Council Offices and the like no doubt and added that Victor had said that Dorsey was friendly with some of these supposed professional men, and they would sometimes meet at Dorsey's place in the evenings.

Dan was taken aback by her response, but tried not to show it and simply said, "so you knew the Dorsey family then?"

"Oh yes, I knew Arnold Dorsey alright, and his father Charles, who was a horrible man, and the apple doesn't fall far from the tree, does it Mr

Nichols".

Dan decided not to push this for the time being and asked how Victor had come to work for Dorsey.

She said Victor had been a very shy and quite sensitive boy. At this point Dan couldn't help noticing a slight hesitation and quiver in her voice and asked if she was OK.

Mrs Collier got up and got herself a glass of water.

This certainly didn't resemble the unhelpful obstructive and quite rude lady they had first encountered, and he began to feel a little sorry for her.

She quickly regained her composure and confirmed that Victor had met Arnold Dorsey when he attended an evening study class of art and Greek mythology. All the other students were young people of similar age to Victor, and she was therefore surprised when she learned that Dorsey, a man in his mid-40's was also a regular attendee.

There were apparently a few young ladies in their late teens and early 20's who also attended the class and Mrs Collier said she didn't trust Dorsey as he was, as she put it" a creep", and wasn't happy that her son was in his company even for this short time and was even more unhappy when Victor told her he had been offered a job at the photographer's studio.

She said she had told her son that the job wouldn't last long, and it didn't, as Victor left after only three months. He never told her why, but Mrs Colliers said she was glad that he had. Then only one month later, Dorsey was found dead, murdered.

She said that Victor went into his shell even further immediately after this and stayed in his room most of the time and then suddenly announced he was leaving and was going to start a new life down South.

"And you haven't heard from him at all, in all those years", Dan asked.

After a little hesitation she said she received just one letter around 3 months after he left simply saying that he was sorry for mistakes he had made and had regretted ever meeting Gerald Dorsey and he should have listened to her warnings.

Dan asked if she still had the letter.

She opened a draw in the sideboard and took out an envelope which bore the tired signs of being opened numerous times. She took out the letter and read it to herself tearfully.

"You see Mr Nichols; my husband was a bully and an alcoholic who had no time for our son. He died when Victor was only 12, alcohol finally taking its toll. Not much of a role model for a young boy I'm sorry to say, and I'm glad we only had the one child", She said.

This was a mother who was clearly missing her son and was worried for his welfare.

Dan asked if she would mind if he saw the letter and Mrs Collier handed it to him, then took another sip of her water.

He read through the single sheet, then laid it flat alongside the envelope and took a photo with his mobile phone.

"I knew Dorsey was trouble she said, he was a womaniser, his father Charles was the same, a "toucher" around females, he made my skin crawl".

Dan looked at his watch and said, *"Our chat has been most helpful Mrs Collier, and I promise that I will keep you informed of our enquiries into Victors present whereabouts, it is important that we speak to him. Just one more question Mrs Collier, did Victor have any close friends who you think he may just have kept in touch with?*

"I have tried to think of that myself Mr Nichols, but to be honest Victor always found it difficult to make friends. I think there was one young lady student at the evening class he seemed to get on with quite well, I think she was foreign, and he mentioned she had a small child, a daughter I think, but I never knew her name, I'm sorry I can't be of more help".

Dan said goodbye and promised he would keep in touch.

There was a lot to digest and process as he headed back to the station.

CHAPTER 14

"Where are you Billy, I have been trying to ring you, but your mobile has been switched off?"

"I'm in Cheetham Hill but on my way back" replied Billy. *"I'll be about half an hour".*

There was a lot to think about in the Dorsey murder case and Dan's "eye for an eye" theory.

He remembered Billy jokingly saying he agreed that aliens may already be here amongst us and mentioning the barman at The Bull. Dan chuckled to himself but couldn't believe he was having a sneaky look around at people as he entered the station and wondered.

"Busy day all round then Danny boy eh" Billy said as they both settled at their desks.

"Pretty constructive talk with Victor Collier's mother Rose", Dan replied.

"Tell me more Dan, while our faithful IT assistant here gets some coffee for these two old men, eh? and see if you can spot Miranda at the same time eh Shivi?"

Dan then proceeded to go through the full, quite amiable chat he had with Rose Collier, which had produced quite a lot of surprising information.

"A difference attitude today then? it must have been your magnetic charm Dan, so the late Arnold Dorsey wasn't very well thought of eh, that's something we didn't know".

"There's a few things I think may be well worth following up Billy, we can let Shivi have a look at the letter and envelope Victor Collier sent to his mother and see if he can get the postal district it was sent from, that at least may give us a starting point.

Also, if we could find out who this young foreign woman was who was a student at the evening class where Victor met her. The study class may even still be active, who knows."

Dan suddenly stopped mid-sentence and said, *"hang on, Collier's alibi was confirmed by a friend, a lady with a foreign name",* He routed through the statements again and said, ***"Krystna Bartosz"****, and we have her address".*

"And what's all this about Dorsey's "cronies" meeting at the studio regularly in the evenings I wonder, Shivi has been working on producing a comprehensive list of his regular clients, which includes some names shown from the Town Hall and Council Offices, maybe these could be some of Dorsey's "cronies" Rose Collier was referring to?" Billy said.

"I need to go through all the statements again Billy and compare with the names shown in Dorsey's booking diary, these could well some of the same people Victor Collier's mother was referring to, Dan said.

"And we can see if Shivi has done the Dorsey family tree, and also find out if Dorsey had made a will". Dan added.

"Plenty for Shivi to get on with, once boy wonder gets back with our coffee, he's probably hanging about hoping to accidentally bump into this Miranda", Billy said.

"Anyway, what's the connection to Cheetham Hill Billy?"

"There isn't one Danny boy, I've found Angus's concertina, I put a few feelers out, funny how a couple of people from my old Bobby days remember the odd favour.

There always used to be places where stuff that had been nicked could be found. Anyway, I got word that an old concertina might be available in Cheetham Hill.

"When I arrived at the place, a tatty old junk shop, I remembered I had been there once before to recover some stolen items, and was surprised it was still open for business, and still had the same name displayed above the shop, **"Honest John, Almost New Antiques".**

A contradiction in terms, his name isn't John, he's a little Jewish fella called Maurice, or as the local drug dealers and the artful dodgers know him, Fagin, ***and*** *he certainly isn't honest, he would sell his own mother for a few shekels.*

I asked Maurice what he wanted for the old squeezebox in the corner at the back of the shop, he gave me a load of bull shit about it coming from a very famous family of Italian musicians. He said he would have to look in his records to see how much he had paid for it.

I told him I was a customer some years back and knew he would look after his old clientele.

He dug out an old thread bare leather-bound ledger from inside his desk draw and thumbed through a few pages, then after a short while and a sort of inward whistle through his teeth said, I see I have already had an offer of £120 for this rare item, but my love and passion for accordion music won't allow me to sell it for that, I wouldn't be able to sleep at night.

I told him I couldn't afford to pay over £120 and started to walk away.

He then said, rubbing his chin in thought, hang on, did you say you were a previous customer? well maybe I could make an exception then, I take it you are local, and I will be seeing you in my shop again?

I said to him, yes, I am indeed local, and oh yes you will be seeing me again in your good as new antique shop, and very soon.

He didn't know how to react to that, and that is when I pulled out my ID.

I said, now I would like to have a look at your sales ledger Maurice and took it from him. He just stood there without another word.

As the shrewd businessman he was, all the items he had bought were logged, along with the dates and prices he had paid. Also, alongside each purchase there was a code, which I assumed identified the seller, no actual names, but numbers and a capital letter of the alphabet after the number.

I made a note of the date the concertina appeared at the shop, which tied in within a day of the date Angus's had his stolen, and I noted Maurice's identification code recorded alongside: 289D.

It was also noticeable that this exact same code and number appeared quite frequently, so I took a shot of two or three previous pages of the ledger on my mobile phone. The guy who snatched old Angus's squeezebox was clearly a regular customer of Fagin's "antique" shop.

I confiscated the concertina and told Maurice I would be back to have a chat with him soon. He started to say, you can't do that, I will call the Police, then realised what he had said, and asked if we can come to some arrangement.

I told him to listen very carefully, as this will be the arrangement. I need to know everything about 289D and I mean everything, and I would call back soon for the information. I said I think you can work out what the alternative arrangement will be.

"So did you take the concertina back to Angus?", Dan asked.

"No, I'm hanging on to it until I know who the scum bag is who nicked it, then I'll reunite the wheezing squeeze box with its rightful owner" Billy replied.

"Blimey, as you say Billy, a busy day all round," said Dan.

"Just thinking, do you fancy a quick half at the Bull tonight Danny boy?" Billy said, "it is Friday after all."

"What? the same Bull as the Bull Shit around the corner, the one you said you couldn't stand?

"Well, I just thought, you know as you have never been in there before, you can see what I mean, and you won't have to take my word for it" Billy replied.

"Whatever Billy, Dan said, looking through the stack of paperwork Shivi had put on his desk, deciding there was no point in trying to figure out Billy's thinking sometimes. *"I am going through all the statements from those who were listed as Dorsey's clients and possible cronies".*

There was a quiet spell in the office as the three-man review team each concentrated on their own various tasks.

The silence was broken as DI Morris arrived. *"Just to let you know lads that the media announcement about this cold case review is being made to the press later today, it will be in the local newspapers from tomorrow, so expect your workload to increase as calls start coming in on Monday. Have a good weekend".*

He then disappeared as quickly as he arrived.

All three looked down at their growing individual workload, then turned to each other with expressions ranging from "what?" to "oh no".

Dan said, *"well I suppose a swift half in the Bull Shit tonight somehow doesn't sound that bad now".*

CHAPTER 15

The Bull was busy considering it was only just after 7, but it was a Friday night.

Obviously one of those pubs where people, mostly men, like to stand at the bar with their drinks, although there were quite a few seated in little groups.

The two old pals found a gap at the bar and Billy ordered the beers.

"Blimey, the barman's a bit of a giant, I bet he comes in handy at throwing out time", Dan said.

"Big Nigel, oh yea, but don't be fooled by appearances Danny boy, he's more likely to knit you a cardigan if you got talking to him nicely", Billy replied.

"Like that is it?" Dan said as he looked around the unfamiliar room. He didn't recognise anyone from the station, but given the short time he had been there, that wasn't surprising. Billy on the other hand received a few nods of recognition from a couple of fellas presumably from his PC days.

Billy was also looking around the room, but Dan thought with a bit more purpose.

"Looking for anyone in particular?"

"What?" Billy replied, still looking all around the room.

"Are you looking for anyone in particular Billy?" Dan repeated very slowly.

"Oh, no, no one in particular" Billy said, still looking around.

Billy suddenly came back to life. *"Well blow me down with your hairdryer Dan, look over there in that corner, it's Eve, you know Peter Knight's sister, what a surprise"*.

"Oh really, a surprise is it Billy? just a swift drink in the Bull was it, just because I have never been in here before?" Dan said rolling his eyes.

"Come on, we'll have to go over and at least say hello Dan".

Billy grabbed his arm and Dan reluctantly had little choice.

"I should have known you were up to something when you mentioned

coming in here tonight" Dan whispered through clenched teeth as they approached the small table in the corner.

The two ladies were sat quietly chatting when Billy approached and said, *"Well, fancy seeing you in here Eve, what a nice surprise. This is my old pal from school days Dan Nichols. You probably won't remember him, but we were at school with your Peter.*

Dan, this is Eve, Peter Knight's sister, you remember Peter Knight don't you Dan?

Dan just nodded in reply, inwardly saying, *"before you go to bed".*

"Yes, nice to meet you ladies" he finally said.

"Can we get you ladies a drink" Billy said, eyeing up the two extra empty chairs at the small table. *"Gin and Tonic's by the looks of it is it?"* as he put his beer on the table and started to turn to go to the bar.

"Let me go and get the ladies drinks Billy", Dan said, jumping at the opportunity to get away.

"No, I insist Dan, you stay and chat, Gin and Tonics on the way ladies", Billy said smiling and heading for the bar.

"You swine Billy", Dan said to himself as he stood by the table with his beer in his hand like a spare part, not knowing what to do next.

After an uncomfortable silence Eve said, *"why don't you sit down Dan,".*

"I thought you may be expecting other friends" Dan said awkwardly sitting himself down at the table and inwardly cursing Billy. He was now sat uncomfortably opposite two ladies he didn't even know and had never met before.

As a retired Military man who had never married and spent most of his army career in the Intelligence Corps, Dan was by profession and nature a quiet and cautious man when meeting people, especially females.

"Eve said, *no, a quick after work chat, just the two of us Dan", this is Paula, we work in the same office at the station. Paula only started here two months ago from working in London, so she doesn't really know many people yet".*

"Oh, well nice to meet you Paula" Dan said, thinking where the hell is Billy? I bet he is taking his time with the drinks on purpose.

"So, you and Billy grew up together here in Manchester then?" Eve said.

"Yes, we joined the army as young lads on the same day, but lost touch as our postings took us on different military career paths and we only met up again after I retired around 18 months ago, so I guess I don't' know many people here either." Dan replied.

Paula was just about to say something when Eve said, *"Paula lost her husband 4 years ago, he was in the Military she has been working in London but decided to come back to her roots in the north".*

Paula just smiled and took a sip of her drink.

Billy finally arrived with two G n T's and sat himself down at the table, raised his glass and said, *"Cheers ladies".*

"Is the Bull your regular then Eve?". Billy asked.

Hardly the simple reply expected, Eve spent the next almost 10 minutes to explain that she only calls into the Bull on a Friday occasionally after work, as she was so busy most of the time, with her many other friends and activities, but she knew how much it helped Paula.

Without stopping, she then went on to explain exactly what she *does* do the rest of the week, day by day, hour by hour in painstaking detail. Even Billy couldn't get a word in.

Billy slurped the last dregs from his glass, looked at his watch and said, *"Gosh, look at the time, we must move on Eve",* much to the relief of Dan, and they suspected to the relief of her friend Paula who had sat in silence throughout.

"I was just thinking Eve, I wondered if you and Paula may like a change and call in at the Golden Ball one Friday night, we all have a laugh as it is open mike night, and there may be people you have not seen for a while, and Paula may enjoy it as well".

"I'd have to check my schedule and see what I've got on, Fridays I sometimes have other commitments", Eve said, then started to list the many options she had on Fridays. Billy quickly interrupted and said, *"Well just let me know Eve".*

As the two men got up Dan said, *"Billy is the DJ and he sings a few songs as well, I'm sure you would enjoy it".*

On their way out of the bar Billy said, *"See the little fella stood chatting at the bar, the one with black curly hair and short beard? he's a local reporter, Eddie Frost, apparently, he's always hanging about, sniffing for inside info hoping to get an exclusive for his paper. I'm told he's a smarmy sod so avoid him Danny boy, rumour is he can be ruthless and drop you in the you know what".*

As they got outside Dan said, *"Blimey, Eve isn't backword at coming forward is she Billy? I thought she would never shut up; I doubt we'll see her in the Golden Ball next week".*

"C and A then Sherlock?" Billy said. *"Why not, it is Friday"* Dan replied, as they chatted along the way. *"I actually felt sorry for her friend".*

"Me too Dan. I don't think she opened her mouth; she didn't really get chance did she, fancy only knowing Eve after arriving here eh? Imagine that".

"I don't have to imagine it Billy, I only ***knew you*** *when I got back, so I know how the poor lady feels".*

"I'm not sure how to take that Danny boy" Billy said patting his old pal on the back as the two laughed together.

CHAPTER 16

It was Saturday morning and Dan bumped into his neighbour Simon from the top apartment as they were both collecting their mail in the entrance of the apartment block.

"Have you seen the bit in the paper this morning Dan about an old unsolved murder case being re investigated? I do remember this one, a photographer was found battered to death in his studio. I still had my legal practice back then; it was 10 years ago. We did occasionally take on criminal work, but of course the Police never got to the bottom of this murder, and nobody was ever arrested".

"No, I haven't seen the paper yet Simon" replied Dan.

"Apparently there is a reward of £10.000 being offered for information leading to the arrest and conviction of the killer, let's hope it pays off eh Dan.

"Yes, let's hope so Simon, once a lawyer, always a lawyer, eh?"

If only Simon knew eh.

£10,000 reward, I wonder if Billy knows, Dan thought, so decided to give him a call.

"Billy, don't know if you've seen this morning's paper, but there's a reward being offered in the Dorsey case, that should prompt a few calls, eh?

"I haven't seen the press, but yep, I sort of had the heads up from Mike Morris that it was on the cards, so next week will be busy". Billy said.

"I'm just on my way to Cheetham Hill, I have an appointment with our friendly antiques expert Honest John, so will touch base later. 10- 4."

Dan somehow hadn't imagined his weekends, or even every day to be like this when he decided to retire after a lifetime career in the military, even after the short 12-month spell working for his old army captain at the private security and investigation agency in London.

I wonder what the captain would think if he knew what I had been persuaded to do now Dan thought.

Back in his apartment he decided to try to switch off from work and watch TV. Sods law it was another "ancient aliens" programme which just took him back to his eye for an eye theory, so he switched off and decided to do some work anyway.

He started to go through the statements of the names which were listed as Dorsey's clients.

It was lunchtime and with a cold meat sandwich and a glass of red wine he now felt quite comfortable going over his workload.

Just for the moment he thought back to the previous night at the Bull and couldn't help reflecting how Eve's friend Paula must have felt during their brief meeting.

He tried to remember what she looked like, or even how she had been dressed, but somehow the constant dominance of Eve shrouded any visual memory.

There were witness statements from five men who were staff members of the local Council office and two others whose role were specifically dedicated to The Mayor's office.

Dan read through all seven statements and colour highlighted the things which they all appeared to agree on, which was that their relationship with Mr Dorsey was conducted via their offices, relating to arranging the professional photographic services required to cover various formal events and functions.

Only two had confirmed they had ever been to the studio and that was for the sole purpose of looking at photograph proofs and occasional video footage prior to release and publication. None said they knew Mr Dorsey on a friendly or personal basis.

On reading over the statements again a few times, Dan couldn't help noticing how the parts he had highlighted were so similar in each one, even the use of the same wording. He checked the dates on the statements, and all were taken on different dates at different times and mainly at different locations.

Looking at Dorsey's business diary again, it was clear from the span of dates covered that these same men must have known the photographer consistently for several years, yet none of them said they considered him a friend or knew him on a personal basis and even seemed keen to emphasise that fact.

Dan found all this hard to accept and decided to suggest to Billy that these men should be interviewed again. Shivi could update their current details.

In the folder with all the statements Dan spotted the statement by the foreign lady friend of Victor Collier who was called Miss Bartosz who had confirmed his alibi. When he checked her address, it wasn't too far from where Billy was heading, so he gave him a call.

"Billy, if you get chance, can you check out this address on your way back from Honest Johns. The female friend of Victor Collier who confirmed his alibi was a Krystna Bartosz, a Polish name apparently. It may be useful to see if she might have an idea where we can find him, she may still be in touch with him."

"Leave it with me Sherlock", Billy replied.

Going through the statements again, Dan read over those from the occupants of the properties immediately neighbouring Dorsey's.

The building on one side was used as offices and therefore completely closed after business hours.

The other side however was divided as rented flats over the three floors and statements taken from three separate tenants of the address had independently confirmed that they had witnessed Dorsey's address being visited in the evenings well after the studio had closed.

The records showed that the Police had checked for any CCTV footage in the immediate area at the time and although there were a few cameras in operation, none were concentrated specifically on the studio frontage.

At least this seemed to confirm there was some truth in Rose Collier's comments that Victor had told her that some of Dorsey's supposed gentlemen friends regularly visited the studio in the evenings.

Just then Billy rang, *"I'm on my way back Dan, we can meet up and have a coffee at that little café near your place".*

"Great, how did you go on Billy?"

"I'll fill you in over coffee. Looks like we may be making some headway at

least Dan".

Dan was able to get a small table outside the café, and Saturday afternoon didn't seem too bad after all as he leaned back in his chair catching the pleasant sunshine on his face waiting for Billy.

His mind again drifted back to the previous evening at the Bull, or the Bull Shit as he was sure Billy would think of it again after their experience with Eve.

That poor friend Paula, she was the complete opposite to Eve, but sometimes self-confident characters like Eve purposely look for quiet maybe even shy people to associate with, as they don't like too much competition.

Dan closed his eyes in the now warm sunshine and again tried to remember what Paula looked like. She was a bit shorter than Eve, and had a neat close-cut hairstyle, sort of hazel colour. Just as he thought he had a full picture in his mind his concentration was abruptly broken by Billy's voice, *"Wakey wakey sleeping beauty".*

"I bet you were stretched out on a beach in Benidorm in the Spanish sunshine then eh Danny Boy?"

"Actually, I was trying to remember what Eve's friend Paula looked like, but I can't get passed Eve's monologue. So, is Benidorm your kind of holiday then Billy?

"I'd rather walk round town with a nail in my shoe Danny boy". Billy replied.

Enjoying the coffee and sunshine in the open air, Dan said, *"How did your meeting with Honest John go?"*

"I told you first I would find the concertina, that was stage one, stage two was to find out who nicked it, now I have the name and some details of that person courtesy of little Maurice, who was keen to maintain his local reputation by avoiding a Police raid on his shop in broad daylight", Billy explained.

"So, what's stage three then Billy?"

"Watch this space Danny boy" he said taking a sip of his coffee and looking rather pleased with himself, *"I'll keep you posted".*

Dan went on to explain his thoughts after having read the witness statements of Dorsey's clients from the Council and Mayor's Offices and those from the neighbouring residential building.

"I think there could have been more going on at Dorsey's place than just photography Billy, and what about the bundle of cash? I wonder if Dorsey had a card school going in the evenings, and he was the banker, we should see if we can speak to some of these people again, what do you think Billy?

"Agreed Dan, we'll get Shivi on it on Monday to get some updates".

"So, did you manage to have a look at that address of Victor Collier's female friend Billy, the Polish lady?

"I did Dan, it's in flat land, the address was apparently let as student accommodation back 10 years ago.

It's still in flats now, but not for students. Mainly DHSS from what I could gather, but a stroke of luck, one of the tenants here, a lady called Carol, confirmed that she was a student tenant back then and had been allowed to keep the tenancy all this time.

Not only that, but this Carol remembers the Polish girl Krystna, they were both students. They weren't best friends, but they did hang out together just occasionally".

"What were the odds of that eh? that was really lucky, tell me more Billy", did she remember Victor Collier as well?"

"Well, it seems Krystna fell pregnant and gave birth to a daughter. She wasn't able to continue her academic life as a student, but listen to this Dan, the landlord allowed her to stay in the flat with her little girl, and there was rumour at the time that the landlord could even be the child's father, although he was thought to be a married man".

"What about Collier, did your informant Carol know him as well Billy?

"Calm down Danny boy, I'm coming to that. She remembered that Krystna used to attend an evening class, and a young man called Victor would pick her up and drop her off home afterwards, Carol had also wondered later if Victor could have been the father of the little girl.

She said that she used to baby sit the young daughter Hanna on the evenings Krystna was at her class and although she didn't really know the *chap Victor, she said he was always very quiet and polite and as far as she knew, he didn't seem to stay overnight."*

She said that Krystna had later found a daytime job where she could take little Hanna with her, she thought it could have been a cleaning job, but that only lasted a few months, and shortly after that she moved out of the flat and Carol never saw her again. Little Hanna would have been aged around 4 or 5 by then".

"You have been busy for a Saturday then Billy, at least we have a bit more information to follow up, strange that Collier and his friend Krystna both seem to have made themselves scarce shortly after Dorsey's murder, eh?

"I think Shivi will find his workstation will be red hot on Monday, what with what we will be now firing at him, as well as a possible feedback response from the media release and offer of ten grand for new information.

Better enjoy your Sunday tomorrow then Danny boy, get some of that relaxing piano music on your antiques roadshow portable radio player, and remember, you will always have an interested ear from Honest John if you ever want to sell it." Billy said.

"Speaking of Honest John, can't you give me just a snippet of what you have already found out about the fella who nicked Angus's accordion Billy, just to get me through the weekend"?

"Oh, OK Dan, just for you, this young fella who is considered a bit of a master of his art locally, and who is revered as a role model by all the young budding arseholes in the area, is known affectionately as ***The Toad*** *as he is said to be too slippery to get caught, he's even got* ***TOAD*** *tattooed on the back of his right hand.*

Stage three will result in The Toad very soon being known as The Turd once my operation ***Toad in the Hole*** *is fully complete, the hole being a shit hole".* Billy said with a broad smile.

CHAPTER 17

A typical overcast Manchester Monday morning, after what had been a quite sunny weekend and the three-man review team gathered at their office, which by now really looked like a busy working office with all three work areas full of paperwork.

The phone was ringing almost immediately with Shivi answering with surprising proficiency after such a short time in the job.

He filled out a separate form detailing all the incoming information from each person who had responded to the media appeal released over the weekend, and by mid-morning the individual forms were increasing.

D I Morris arrived looking quite upbeat, repeating his sometimes-annoying habit of rubbing his hands together like he was just about to devour his favourite cream cake.

"I understand the public responses have been coming in already gents, so I look forward to getting an update from you. I know you have been busy reviewing all the original findings over the past few weeks, and you have been to see the pathologist Dr Armstrong, so push on gents and I will see you in my office tomorrow at 4pm, "He said, rubbing his hands together again as he left.

"I bet he's got a vanilla slice or something waiting for him back in his office" Dan said rubbing his hands together mocking their boss.

The phone continued to ring, and Shivi's forms continued to grow.

"We will divide the forms between us later Dan and try to assess what we think we can follow up on, let's hope there is someone out there who genuinely knows something eh?" Billy said.

Shivi chipped in, *"from what I've got here on some of the forms so far, your prediction could well be right about the likely fruits and nuts getting in touch Billy.*

"Oh, and Shivi, Billy managed to get to the address of Victor Colliers lady friend Krystna Bartosz on Saturday, but she left the address years ago, can you throw her name into the pot when searching for social media

platforms etc. to see if she can be located. And we know she has a daughter called Hanna who will be a teenager by now so that may help".

"And we need you to update the details of the witnesses who worked at the Council and Mayors office and gave statements, there are seven of them, I've put their statements in a file for you, we want to interview them again". Dan continued.

"You know Dan, along with what we already planned to do, we will have some of the people from the public appeal to see and interview, most I suspect will be happy to come into the station, but I honestly think we are going to need help".

"I hadn't thought about that Billy, how will we get round that?" Dan asked.

"I'm going to see if the boss can give us some help, just to get through this immediate workload, I'll have a word with him before we see him tomorrow afternoon" Billy replied.

"In the meantime, let's have a look through some of Shivi's forms, I will bet you here and now Dan there will be a few weirdos who will claim to know who the killer is and exactly why they did it.

By the end of the day, they had divided the forms in the categories of *Possible, Unlikely and Ridiculous.*

"Let's get rid of the weirdos first eh Dan" Billy said, "listen to this one from a fella from Moston.

I have been watching this American TV show about real murders and I have guessed who the murder was every single time in every episode. If you let me have the names of the people you think it might be, I guarantee I will pick the right one. PS I am happy to split the reward with you.

After a couple of equally stupid responses Dan said, *"There's one here from a female who says she worked as a cleaner for Dorsey and has information which she says is significant but wishes to remain anonymous. She has left a mobile number; shall I follow that one up Billy?"*

"Yep, you do that Danny boy, you seem to have a bit more success on your own, maybe I still smell of an ex-copper eh? anyway there's an interesting one here from a fella called Bob Smith who hasn't left any address or contact details but says he will meet at Piccadilly Station tomorrow at

2pm, on the bench near the entrance to platform 14".

I'll have a go at that one Dan, we have a meet up with D I Morris in his fancy office at 4pm tomorrow remember".

"I will see if I can get in touch with this anonymous female in the meantime and see, or hear what she has to say, it would be good if we had some positive info to report eh? Dan said.

Whilst all this was going on, Shivi was quietly getting on with his other areas of research and suddenly said, *"I think I may have picked up something on Kyrstna, well on a young teenager by the name of Hanna Bartosz on a social media platform, it's sort of pointing towards her possibly being in the London area, I've got a few more things I can try".*

"Well done Shivi", Billy said,*" keep it up, if it is the daughter they may still be in touch with Collier".*

"That's the connection I am looking for, there are a few names I can see she has been in touch with quite recently, so fingers crossed", Shivi replied, clearly enjoying the challenge.

"Another thing Billy, are any of the detective team who worked on this case still around now, I mean at this station? Dan asked.

"Looking through the witness statements we have, I don't personally recognise any of them, but it's likely a Specialised Homicide Squad from another Force was brought in, I guess we could ask the boss tomorrow" Billy said, "anyway, coffee time I think eh lads?"

Over coffee, Billy suddenly said,*"what's your ambition Shivi, I mean what do you want to achieve in life?"*

"Blimey, where did that come from?" Dan said.

"Well come on Shivi, you are twenty-one in a couple of weeks, do you want to be in the Police Force all your working life and rise the ladder of ranks, or travel the world maybe, or do something else? Billy continued.

"Where's all this philosophical stuff coming from all of a sudden Billy? Dan said.

"Well by the time we were twenty-one we were in the Army, it seemed like we were barely out of school, and look at us now Dan, what have we achieved eh?"

"Blimey, is it annual depression day? We both did OK, look at you Billy, you were captain of the Crown and Anchor's winning darts team two years on the trot, you have a captivated admiring audience every first Friday of the month at the Golden Ball, and you were a well-respected Police Constable in this part of the Manchester community, and you did travel a bit during your Army career, ***and*** *I remember you won the school egg and spoon race one year".*

Poor Shivi, just sat in silence wondering what to think, then assuming he was expected to answer Billy's question said,

"Yes, I would like to see more of the world, especially India, and I suppose I would like to make a success of my Police career, but I know I could never achieve the leadership level of some officers who are considered iconic figures in the Police Force, some even referred to as indispensable".

Dan said, *"let me share something with you"* and reached into his pocket and pulled out his wallet, both Shivi and Billy wondering what he was doing. He took out a folded piece of paper that looked as though it hadn't seen daylight for years.

He unfolded the paper and said, *"let me read you something that I first heard when I was at a Sunday School concert in the Church Hall when I was 14.*

It made an impression on me that day, enough for me to shyly approach the man who read it out at the end of the concert and ask him if I could take a copy and write it down.

The man said, I will do better than that young man, here take this. He folded his paper up and gave it to me, adding I know it off by heart.

I have never forgotten that man and have kept this copy ever since, and over the years, just occasionally, I dig it out and read it, just as a reminder".

By now he had the full attention of both Shivi and Billy as Dan began to slowly read.

Some time when you're feeling important
Some time when your ego's in bloom
Some time when you take it for granted
You're the best qualified man in the room
Some time that you feel that your going

Would leave an unfillable hole
Just follow these simple instructions
And see how they humble your soul
Take a bucket and fill it with water
Put your hands in it up to your wrists
Pull them out and the hole that remains
Is the measure of how much you'll be missed
You may splash all you please when you enter
You may stir up the waters galore
But stop! And you'll find in a minute
That it looks just the same as before.
The moral of this is quite simple
You must do the best that you can
Be proud of yourself but remember
There is no indispensable man.

There was a long silence before Billy finally said, *"Well that's sorted me out then eh? but you are right Danny boy, I was being a bit of a miserable sod wasn't I, probably Monday blues, and I did win the egg and spoon race. Anyway, that sounds like good advice, what do you think Shivi?*

Shivi said, *"Can I take a copy of that Dan please?"*

"I will do better than that young man, Dan replied, *"here take this, I know it off by heart Shivi"* and folded the ageing bit of paper back up and handed it to Shivi with a wide smile and a knowing wink.

"That was a very nice gesture today Dan" Billy said as the two men walked out of the station after what had been another interesting day.

"Tomorrow is another day eh Billy' so no more Monday blues eh" Dan said and put a friendly arm around his old pal's shoulder as they walked on their way.

CHAPTER 18

Preparing for the days planned tasks on their way into the office Billy's thoughts were on meeting with a Bob Smith at Piccadilly train station, whilst Dan was to follow up on information from an anonymous female who claimed to have some new information re the Dorsey murder.

Shivi was already busy at his workstation when they arrived. *"Good morning gents"* he said in a cheery voice.

"You sound happy this morning Dan said, *"have you won the lottery or something?*

"Or maybe he saw Miranda on the way in this morning" Billy said.

"I've got some interesting news, Shivi said, "I'm pretty sure I've got the general area where Hanna Bartosz and her mother Krystna are located, everything is pointing towards somewhere around Brixton, London".

"That's interesting," Dan said, "Collier's mother said Victor was going to start a new life down South, just a thought, I could see if the captain can help".

"The captain?" Shivi enquired.

"When I finished in the Army Shivi, I spent 12 months working for my old Captain who had set up a private security and investigation company in London before I finally retired for good and came back to Manchester" Dan replied.

"I don't think that will be necessary Dan; we do have a Police Force in London you know" Billy said.

"Yeh, but the captain's company deal mainly with civil matters, not the kind of things that the Police get involved with or are even aware of". Dan said.

"What kind of things do you mean Dan?", Shivi asked.

"Well, lots of other non-criminal stuff, debt related issues, insurance claims investigation, matrimonial stuff" Dan said, *"lots of information is gathered from that kind of work that the Police will not be aware of".*

"I'll give you that Danny boy, the captain certainly helped with some of the stuff we were dealing with a few months ago".

"What kind of stuff was that?" Shivi asked.

"We can tell you another time Shivi" Billy said, *"we've got enough work to do at the moment".*

"I'll leave you to check the Council workers statements again Dan when you've made contact with your mysterious anonymous cleaning lady", Billy said, "I'm off to Piccadilly to meet with this Bob Smith and don't forget we've got to see D I Morris later, and Shivi keep digging into this possible location in London for the Bartosz female".

"10 - 4 boss", Shivi said, as Dan and Billy looked at each other and smiled.

Piccadilly station was packed as usual with people arriving and others waiting for their departure trains, travellers rushing in opposite directions trailing suitcases and somehow managing not to bump into each other.

Billy made his way to the area directly opposite the check in gate for platform 14 and plonked himself down on an empty form.

The message from Bob Smith was to meet at 2 pm and Billy's watch was showing 1. 50pm. By the time it was 2.10pm Billy was getting twitchy with no sign of the informant. Probably some weirdo who gets a kick out of wasting Police time he thought and decided to wait until 2.15pm, then call it a day.

He looked at the nearby mingling crowd and noticed a chap who had been hanging around occasionally looking at his watch. From a distance there was something familiar about him.

CHAPTER 19

Back at the office Dan had called the mobile number for the lady who had made contact in response to the public appeal. It took a few attempts before anyone replied.

The female who eventually answered said in a whisper she only had a few minutes to speak and was not prepared to come to the Police station but would be prepared to meet with Dan by arrangement on the understanding that she had an absolute assurance that her identity remained anonymous.

Because of the initial delay in getting through to the lady, Dan asked if there was a more convenient time when he could call again. She hurriedly said he could call her at again tonight at 9pm, and quickly terminated the call.

Billy arrived back from his meeting at Piccadilly with about 10 minutes to go before their meeting with DI Morris.

"How did you get on with Mr Smith Billy" Dan said.

"I'll tell you later Dan, anyway, how did your efforts go? whoops let's have a proper catch up later, eh?" Billy said looking at the time. *"Come on, we need to see the boss, you know what he's like, by now, he'll be watching the clock, and we can't upset his cream cake timetable can we".*

"Was he always, well, portly?" Dan said.

"You mean overweight Dan, Mike was quite slim when he was younger, and to be fair was very popular with the ladies in the station" Billy replied.

As they made their way upstairs to DI Morris's office Dan said, *"did you get chance to ask if we could get some manpower help in dealing with these new incoming calls from the public appeal?".*

"Yes, he said he would sort something out for us, let's see what he has to say Dan".

As they reached the corridor at the top of the stairs, they almost bumped into two ladies who had just come out of the typing pool and politely stepped to one side to let the ladies' pass.

"It's Dan, isn't it? and Billy" the first one said.

As they looked up it was Eve's friend Paula with another lady. *"Nice to see you again Paula" Billy said, "Oh yes and me too" Dan said".*

The men walked on, then both turned and glanced back at the ladies, just as Paula had also turned around and smiled. *"What do you think Danny boy?" Billy said with a wink and a grin.*

"Well actually she seemed quite nice" Dan replied. *"Good job Eve wasn't with her then eh?* Billy said sarcastically.

"Come on in gents" DI Morris greeted them and gestured them to take a seat. *"Tell me you have got some good news lads eh?"*

Billy took control and explained that they were certainly making good progress and the recent batch of information coming in from the public appeal was being processed and they had two informants they were particularly interested in but didn't mention names and said they should have updates on these two in the next few days.

Billy also stressed that Shivi was coping well with the other avenues of research and in summary, things were progressing well with just a three-man team.

"On that note, is it likely we will get some help to get through these latest batch of informants?" Billy said.

"All organised, don't worry, Detective Constable Sam Brown, will be starting with you tomorrow. Sam is an experienced detective and particularly good at conducting interviews". DI Morris concluded.

On their way back downstairs Dan said, *"I thought you would have mentioned your meeting with this Bob Smith".*

"Not yet, slow down Sherlock, I wanted to hear about your anonymous female cleaner, let's just see how Shivi is going on, then maybe a catch up at the C & A later eh?".

"Sounds like a plan to me Watson" Dan replied.

Shivi was just packing away and shutting down his workstation.

"You managed without us for a few hours then eh?" Billy said. "Any other conscientious members of the Manchester community come forward with

new information?"

"Just a couple Billy but looks like they could be from the fruit and nut brigade". Shivi replied.

"But remember I told you I thought I had narrowed it down to where Krystna Bartosz and her teenage daughter may be located from some of their social media activity, well it could just tie in with the post mark on that envelope that Victor Collier's mother showed to Dan, so they could be in the same location or even be together. I've just got a couple of other things I can try tomorrow to be more confident". Shivi said.

"Well, that is just tickety boo Shivi, well done, and tomorrow you'll be pleased to know we will have some help from DC Sam Brown, the boss tells me he is a very experienced detective, so see you in the morning". Billy said.

After Shivi had left both men had another look through their notes before setting off for a catch up at the pub.

After a short silence Dan said, *"Who would have thought we would be doing this at our age after all these years?"*

"What, planning to have a beer with an old school mate?"

"No, I mean trying to get to the bottom of an old unsolved murder". Dan replied.

"Hey, speaking of old school mates, I found a couple of old black and white photos the other night, I'll have to show you, Dougie, our friendly landlord of the Golden Ball and some others in our class, I'm sure you will remember some of them". Billy said.

"As long as you don't mention Peter Knight again", Dan replied waving his finger.

"You know Dougie was really funny at school, he still is", Billy continued. "When he first took over at the Golden Ball, we had a little sort of two Ronnies comic routine going at the bar".

"What do you mean, routine?" Dan asked.

"Well, I would say something like, *"Does your young niece still play the mouth organ?* and Dougie would say, *"you mean our Monica? and I would say, "no the mouth organ",* then I would just walk away with a straight face, and he would carry on serving the drinks while the others at the bar just looked at each other not knowing what to think.

I've just remembered another" Billy continued, Dougie would say, *"Shame those three walkers were killed in separate incidents climbing that peak in the Lakes",* and I would say, *"Yes, strange that all three were called Walker".*

Just then Billy's mobile rang, it was DI Morris. Billy listened intently.

It's the boss, he wants to see me now, and it sounds urgent" he said. "You go on and I'll catch you up in the C n A Dan".

CHAPTER 20

Now sat on his own in their usual corner Dan wondered what could be so important that DI Morris had to summon Billy.

He decided to go over what had developed over the past few days and started to make a list of some of the stuff they hadn't yet covered while he was waiting for Billy.

Had Dorsey made a will. Did Shivi produce Dorsey's family tree?

Shivi had done some research which indicated there were no named close relatives, and as for who owned the studio building, it turns out that Dorsey had borrowed heavily on the property and there were several legal charges, basically showing that banks and a building society owned the building. He had probably invested much more in the investment scam than they knew.

Just then Billy arrived and had his serious face on. *"I think I'll get us a large scotch Dan; I think we'll need one"* he said before sitting down.

"Well come on, what was so urgent Billy?" Dan asked.

"You're not going to believe this Dan, a small package arrived at the station a few hours ago. Inside the package was an old tin box, and wait for it, inside the tin box was a single tooth".

The two men stared at each other in silence for a minute before Billy said, *"a tooth for a tooth?".*

"Blimey, what did the boss think Billy?

"Well remember, we hadn't even mentioned your possible theory to him up to this point Dan, but I did tell him what you had Dr Armstrong confirm that the tooth was nowhere to be found at the scene, and your possible biblical explanation. Anway, the package and the contents are now at the forensics lab for analysis, everything will be checked for prints etc. and the tooth itself I assume will be checked to see if it was Dorsey's.

"Was there no note or anything with the package?" Dan said.

"No note, but inside the little tin the tooth was wrapped in a bit of paper which had just one word written on it, DRAN."

"Dran, what does that means Billy, someone's initials maybe?".

"Hopefully we'll find out more tomorrow when we should have the initial results from the forensic team."

They raised their glasses and Billy said, *"I must admit, I didn't go for this eye for an eye, tooth for a tooth business Dan, but it could be you are right, who else would know about a missing tooth?*

After getting a second drink, and trying to take in this latest information, Dan finally said, *"Well, come on, are you going to fill me in with your meeting with the mysterious fella Smith at Piccadilly station?".*

"OK Dan, I got myself settled on the small bench close to the entrance gate for platform 14, the message was to meet at 2pm. By quarter past there was no show, and I am thinking this Smith is just some time-wasting arsehole. Then I spot a fella who had been hanging around looking at his watch and the station clock. Then when I got a proper look at him, I thought he looked familiar.

He had been looking over to the bench every now and then and that's when I realised who it was. He wouldn't know me, but I knew it was him. I got up from the bench and walked away, then circled behind him.

Billy then took a pause and had a drink of his beer.

Dan was now on the edge of his seat. *"Well come on Billy, who was it?"*

"It was Eddie Frost, Billy finally said.

"Eddie Frost, who the hell is he" Dan said.

"You remember when we were in the Bull the other night and I pointed out a newspaper reporter who is always sniffing around for bits of information the Police might know but have not yet made public? well, it was him". Billy said.

"I vaguely remember him", Dan replied, *"but why would he be there?"*

"I couldn't figure out why he was there either Dan, then it dawned on me, it was a set-up, there wasn't any Bob Smith, it was Headline Eddie hoping the Police Officer who turned up was someone he knew and could start shmoozing up to later to see if he could get any information on how the case was going.

Dan was now really on the edge of his seat. *"What did you do Billy?*

"I walked around and approached him from behind, I passed him then turned around and said, It's Eddie Frost isn't it, the reporter, I thought it was you. It surprised him and he said, do I know you? I said no, probably not, I was a local PC some years ago and have seen you occasionally in the Bull.

Before he had chance to say anything I said, I suppose you are waiting to meet someone for your next news story eh, I suppose that happens all the time in your job.

He looked uncomfortable and said, what did you say your name was? I told him PC Billy Oliver, well I was. I said, maybe your next news story contact hasn't turned up and I'm guessing yours is a tough job and it's important you get exclusive stories.

I could tell in that split second Dan, that he knew he had been bubbled, and that I was aware what he was up to.

I said, tell you what Eddie, let me have your contact number and if I hear of any local newsworthy stories, I give you the nod, and with that I winked and walked away".

"Blimey, I wasn't expecting that, can't he be done for wasting Police time Billy?"

"He certainly can Dan, and he knows that very well, but I have a different idea, I'll tell you later. Anyway, never mind that, what about your anonymous lady phone call?".

"Well, when I finally got through to her on her mobile, she sounded frightened and was speaking in a whisper, it obviously wasn't a convenient time, and she asked if I would ring her again at 9 tonight".

Billy looked at his watch and said, *"you better get a move on then Danny boy, its nearly 8 now. You don't want to be ringing from in here, let's call it a night and get off home, you can ring from the quiet comfort of your place".*

"Good idea Billy, I can give you a call if there is anything of great interest, otherwise, see you in the morning".

On his way into his apartment building his neighbour Tammy was just coming home from her nursing shift. Poor girl Dan thought, she always looks tired, but always has a smile.

"Hello Dan, how are you, I've not seen you for a while, still enjoying your relaxing retirement time with your pal Billy?"

Dan just smiled and nodded.

"Oh, by the way Dan, we may be having a new neighbour moving in downstairs, somebody came to view Kevin Carter's old flat on the ground floor next to Alice. I do hope whoever does take it turns out to be suitable, it will be nice for Alice to have a friendly neighbour", Tammy said as she entered her apartment.

Dan couldn't help reflecting on how Kevin Carter could have played such a despicable a part in the horse charity scam that ripped off even his own elderly neighbour Alice. At least justice was done, and Carter and his cohorts were locked up for their crimes. Dan and Billy themselves had played a major role in uncovering the evidence that got the gang arrested and convicted.

Dan just had time to get himself settled down with a cup of tea before he made the phone call, dead on 9pm as the lady had requested.

The phone only rang once when the lady answered, she must only have this 9pm short window where she feels safe to speak Dan thought.

Dan said, *"Before we speak, I know you wanted to remain anonymous, and that's OK, but my name is Dan, Dan Nichols, and I will have to call you something.*

After a second, she said, *"Well just call me Brenda".*

Dan still had the small digital voice recorder from the time he worked for his old Army Captain's investigation agency in London and had linked the device up to his phone.

The recorder had been successfully used in exposing a horse charity scam when one of Dan's elderly neighbours Alice had been the victim of the huge fraud and had also proved vital when his other neighbour Owen had used it to record his own recollections of meeting a man who turned out to be the criminal who had stolen Owen's dog Brendan.

Over the next 35 minutes Dan let Brenda speak, without interruption being conscious of not asking anything which could be considered as "leading" questions.

She stated that she had once worked for Dorsey as a cleaner at his photographic studio after answering an advert in the local press.

Then what she went on to nervously say, took Dan by total surprise.

Surely, she couldn't be making all this up he thought, it had to be genuine, and Dan was glad he had decided to record the whole telephone conversation.

CHAPTER 21

Billy and Shivi were already at their desks when Dan arrived at the office the next morning.

Billy had just been explaining to Shivi about his trip to meet the non-existent Bob Smith set up attempt by the newspaper reporter Eddie Frost.

"Well, I hope your phone call last night with the anonymous lady was more successful than my wasted time at Piccadilly Station Dan" Billy said.

Dan was just about to explain and was reaching into his case for the little recording machine when a knock came at the door, and a lady appeared. She was smartly dressed in a dark blue business-like skirt and jacket and sparkling white blouse.

"Can I help you madam?" Billy said.

"Good morning gents, Detective Constable Sam Brown, pleased to meet you". She replied.

Shivi said out loud, *"She's a woman".*

"Well, he's sharp isn't he, I can see why he was chosen to be part of your intelligence team" she snapped back in a flash. *"Sorry to disappoint young man, my name is Samantha, but my colleagues call me Sam".* she said to Shivi, who by now was looking decidedly embarrassed at his outburst.

"Welcome aboard DC Brown, or I should say Sam" Billy said with a broad smile and a genuine warm handshake. *"This is Dan, the other member of our little team".*

"Yes, I've heard all about the both of you from DI Morris, pleased to meet you Dan" she said.

"Shivi, why don't you nip to the storage room and grab another chair for Sam", Dan said, then whispered quietly in his ear at the door, *"And make sure it doesn't squeak".*

The formalities now over, Billy explained as best he could how far their research and enquiries had got in this decade old murder case and how they were now needing help with interviewing some of the original witnesses again, plus dealing with some of the possible new information coming in from the recent public appeal.

Shivi arrived back with the extra chair which he had been swivelling around all the way from the storeroom to make sure it didn't squeak. He still looked embarrassed as he politely put the chair down by DC Brown and courteously remained standing whilst she sat down.

"Don't worry Shivi, you're not the first person to find out Sam Brown is a woman, even my husband Dennis remembers sometimes" she said with a wide smile.

Billy laughed out loud and winked at Dan as if to say, I have a feeling DC Sam Brown is going to fit in well with our team.

Detective Constable Sam Brown was Manchester born and bred, her father Jack White was a fireman and her mother Ivy a supervisor at the local Coop store in Ancoats where they lived. Samantha Jane White was their only child.

Sam eventually joined the Manchester Police Force aged 24 as a WPC as was known at that time, and after four years on the beat served a probationary period of two years as a Detective Constable before her permanent moved into plain clothes.

Sam had married Dennis Brown, and she often joked that on the day she wed, she simply changed from White to Brown.

Shivi was still going through Billy and Dan's written observations and was compiling this latest information that a package had arrived late the day before containing a small tin box inside which was a single tooth wrapped in a piece of paper with just the word DRAN written on it.

He was reading it to himself and wondering what the word DRAN could mean, then without realising it, he repeated the word out loud.

Sam looked up from her conversations with Dan and Billy and said to Shivi, *"There's no need to use that kind of language young man, especially in front of a lady".*

Poor Shivi didn't know what he had done wrong again.

"What do you mean Sam, that kind of language?" Dan said.

"DRAN is the Polish word for BASTARD" she replied.

"Polish" Dan and Billy looked at each other. *"How did you know that?"* Billy said.

"Before I had the crazy idea of joining the Police Force, I was studying to become a health worker, a nurse, and during that time I had a spell of working in the evenings as a waitress in a Polish restaurant here in Manchester. I learnt a few choice words listening to the kitchen staff I can tell you. They didn't say, **oh dear** *when they accidentally cut a finger or caught a hand on a hot stove".*

"How long have you been in the Police", Shivi asked.

"Is that your polite way of asking how old I am Shivi" she said.

"Oh no, no Sam" he replied apologetically, thinking he had again said the wrong thing.

"Don't worry Shivi, I'm only winding you up, you will soon get used to my sense of humour" she said with an assuring smile.

The phone rang, *"Its DI Morris, he wants to see you and Dan in his office Billy",* Shivi said.

"You carry on going through everything with DC Brown here while we pop upstairs, Billy replied, *"and see if you can learn a few more swear words in Polish from Sam",* Billy said.

"What do you think of Detective Constable Sam Brown then Danny boy?" Billy said as they headed for the stairs. *"I can see why she is considered a confident and capable cop, and she's got a sharp sense of humour for sure".*

"Well, I can't argue with that Billy, I like her, she certainly got Shivi weighed up straight away, I felt really sorry for him when he asked how long she had been in Police, and she snapped back at him about her age".

Just before they reached the boss's office Dan said, *"I've still not told you how my 9m pm phone call last night went with this lady Brenda.*

"Oh so at least we know her name now then Dan".

"How's things going with DC Sam Brown then lads?" Milke Morris said.

"For her first day she has certainly made an instant impression, and as you

said, she is certainly smart, and I suspect doesn't suffer fools. She will fit in well, and Shivi is continuing to bring her up to speed with where we are at this stage", Billy replied.

"Now this package that arrived last night, the lab has confirmed that the tooth is human and not animal, and further tests are being carried out to confirm if it did belong to Dorsey, we should get that result tomorrow", and then produced a photograph of the package and its contents for Dan and Billy to see.

"The outer package and the little tin, which incidentally is a solid silver snuff box, have produced some fingerprints which are being checked against existing databases and the origin of the little tin, which appears to be quite old is certainly not British, and as you can see from the faint colouring and motif is thought it may possibly come from".

Before he could continue, Billy cut him short and said, ***"From Poland"***, then continued his interruption and said, *"and the piece of paper the tooth was wrapped in with the Polish word DRAM on it, is the Polish word for **BASTARD**.*

Dan could see this was annoying the Boss who said, *"is there anything else you would like to tell me, like who the fingerprints belong to, or better still who the murderer was, and save everyone else the time?".*

Billy could see he had overstepped the mark and instantly shut up.

Dan quickly said, *"It was actually Sam Brown who told us that Dram was the Polish word for bastard this morning, and Billy was just about to explain that we also have another potential Polish connection".*

Appearing to have diffused the situation for the moment Dan explained their enquiries regarding Victor Collier and his connection at the time of the murder with a young Polish lady called Krystna Bartosz and their ongoing research to locate Collier and Bartosz who were thought to have relocated to the Greater London area shortly after the murder. *"Shivi is working on that now"* Dan continued.

This information seemed to genuinely cool matters and DI Morris stood up, looked at his watch and said, *"Well off you go chaps, that sounds like good news, keep me posted and I'll update you when the other lab tests come in re the tooth and fingerprints".*

Once out of the office Dan said, *"I thought for a minute you had pushed it a bit in there Billy".*

"I think I know Mike pretty well, he's OK, and by the looks of it, it was probably vanilla slice time for him anyway" Billy said.

Passing the typing pool Dan glanced through the corridor windows which didn't go unnoticed by Billy. *"Looking for anyone special Danny boy?".*

Dan didn't bother replying, knowing if he did, Billy wouldn't let it drop.

CHAPTER 22

Back downstairs Shivi and Sam were deep in conversation going through the list of witnesses who would need to be processed and had drawn up a schedule of which ones Sam would interview.

As they entered Dan was just asking Billy about the situation with Angus and the toe rag known as The Toad and wondering how Billy's "Operation Toad in the Hole" was doing.

Sam heard just the tail end of the conversation and said, *"What's this then, a new lead?".*

Dan laughed and said, *"No this has nothing to do with the case, Billy has this old friend with one leg called Angus".*

Sam quick as a flash said, *"what's his other leg called?"*

Shivi almost choked his coffee then all four laughed out loud before eventually settling down.

Billy then explained basically what had happened in their briefing with DI Morris and showed Sam and Shivi the photograph of the package and its contents which had mysteriously arrived at the station.

"This tin is thought to be a snuff box, but as you can see it looks very old and not in the best condition and is possibly from Poland, don't suppose your time working at the Polish restaurant ever came across anything like this Sam?" Billy asked.

"No nothing like that, but I know snuff was popular with some of the people who used to come into the restaurant, and I think maybe one of the older chefs as well, but I've never seen anything like this, it looks almost antique." Sam said.

"I can have a chat to some of the local Polish community and see if anyone recognises the tin if you want" Sam continued.

"No, not at this stage Sam, best keep this to ourselves, you know how word spreads and how some newspaper reporters are for snooping and leaking stories" Billy replied as he glanced over to Dan.

"And we don't want to let this be known without the boss authorising it do

we Billy" Dan said.

"Tomorrow is another day, and Shivi you can do some research to see if anything can be found about this old snuff box. Also, we should get the result of the tests re fingerprints etc. so see you all tomorrow eh". Billy said.

After Sam and Shivi had left, Dan reached into his case and pulled out his digital voice recorder.

"I need you to listen to this Billy, this lady Brenda had some serious things to say about Dorsey and his activity at the photographic studio during my phone call to her, and if what she says is true, this could put a whole new perspective on the murder. Take it home with you and play the whole recording, I think you will be surprised".

Now in the comfort of his home Billy couldn't wait to play back the telephone recording so settled in with a note pad and pen, and poured himself a glass of scotch, then decided to keep the bottle close to hand.

What he heard was unexpected to say the least'.

Tape Recording

(Brenda)

I was aged 22 when I answered an advert in the local paper for a part time cleaner at Dorsey's Studio.

I had been married for just over a year, and we both had good full times jobs with the same small engineering company and had managed to get on the property ladder with our first little terraced house.

One day we were so happy, the very next, we were informed that the company was closing. The firm manufactured component parts for a larger company who supplied the textile industry, and the ultimate client had lost their huge contract to an overseas supplier. We were devastated.

We both immediately started to try to find work, but lots of our friends and former work colleagues were in the same boat and any local work that was going was soon snapped up. We were so worried we couldn't pay our mortgage payments, so I was pleased to get an interview for the cleaning job, even though the advert made it plain it was part time work. My husband Tom on the other hand was unable to find anything.

At the interview I was one of three women present, and whilst waiting I was not very hopeful of getting the job as the other two ladies were much older, and from their brief conversation clearly had previous professional cleaning experience. I was therefore pleasantly surprised to be told immediately by the studio owner Mr Dorsey that I had got the job. Looking back, I suppose this should have told me something, however he was aware of my circumstances, and I thought he had perhaps felt sorry for me.

I was doing all the general cleaning of the ground floor rooms for the first few months, then Mr Dorsey asked if I would occasionally clean his study which was upstairs in his private quarters, as every other week he had business colleagues' round in the evening for a meeting and the next morning the room always needed to be cleaned and tidied. He said he would pay extra for my time, and I naturally agreed.

He showed me into the study which was a quite large room with paintings hung around the walls and lots of books in antique style cabinets. He explained that all the paintings were of Greek Gods and Goddesses and that's why they were mostly naked, there was also an almost life-sized statue of a naked female who he told me was the goddess Aphrodite. He said that he had studied Greek Mythology at college and had a degree.

The study was set out as a sort of classroom type layout with several chairs and small tables at one end. He explained that this was exactly the way the room needed to be set up when she cleaned it the mornings after his meetings. He emphasised that the statue had to be cleaned with a special soft cloth.

On the first occasion I had to do this, I went into the study and the chairs had been left scattered untidily around and there were empty drinks glasses on the tables and the odd glass and ashtray on the floor. Mr Dorsey came in and gave me the soft cloth which had to be used to clean the statue.

I began to tidy the chairs and clean things up, then started to wipe down the statue with the soft cloth. At this point, out of the corner of my eye I saw Mr Dorsey watching me from the doorway and it made me feel a bit uncomfortable.

As I finished off, I thought I detected a smell of perfume in the room but thought no more about it, and I was delighted when Mr Dorsey handed me an envelope with an extra £50.00 cash inside.

The second time I had to clean the study after one of the evening meetings, the room again had been left in a very untidy state with some drink spillages on the floor and empty glasses left around, and on this occasion, I could definitely smell the lingering of perfume.

As I continued clearing everything away, I saw an envelope on the floor under one of the chairs. The envelope was open, and I could see there were photographs inside. I looked around before taking the photographs out and was shocked with what I saw. They were single shots of a young lady posing in various positions, and from the background I could see the photographs had been taken in this very room.

Mr Dorsey entered the room as I was still looking at the photographs and said, oh don't be shocked, this is just part of our evening class where all my colleagues are also studying Greek Mythology, and these ladies are all professional life models and get paid for taking part.

I handed the photographs to him, and he calmly gave me the extra payment of £50.00. I didn't know what to say.

As I was leaving the room he said, have you ever done any modelling, I think you would be equally as good as these other ladies, they get paid very well for just the one evening you know, as much as £300.00 for just one session. Maybe you should think about it, I would be happy to add you to the list. I quickly finished what I was doing and left, still wondering what had just happened.

When I got home Tom was just sat there, he still hadn't had any luck finding a job and it was beginning to tell on him. He had become irritable and argumentative, and to make matters worse there was a letter from the Building Society on the floor beside him, reminding us we were behind with our mortgage and demanding payment by the end of the month, this certainly was not the right time to tell him what I had just experienced.

Even after I showed him the extra money I had just earned, that didn't seem to help, in fact it just made matters worse, and he just sat there without speaking.

That night I struggled to sleep and couldn't stop thinking about Mr Dorsey's comment that these life models could be paid as much as £300.00 just for a few hours work in the evening and by the morning I had made my mind up.

The next day I told Mr Dorsey that I would do the next model session as I needed the money if I was paid £300.00 and that's how it started.

I did several evening "meetings" after that, telling Tom I was serving drinks etc. for Dorsey's business colleagues.

After a while I began to justify this to myself as simply doing a job. There were plenty of Manchester night clubs where there were lap dancing bars and waitresses were going around serving drinks topless, at least nobody here ever touched me, just looked and took photographs, and I was paying the mortgage by taking cash into the Building Society and this took the pressure off Tom.

Then out of the blue Tom had been offered a job taxi driving, mainly doing the Manchester Airport run but it changed his life after months of depression and our marriage was getting back on track.

The taxi work grew, and Tom was doing more hours around the town centre. Then one night he had a call to collect a couple of men from Dorsey's address. They had both had had a few drinks and were chatting and laughing on the journey home. The next day when he was cleaning out the back of his cab Tom found an envelope on the floor. He thought it may contain something which might identify the owner, as he had done quite a few pick-ups during that night, but regretfully inside the envelope were naked photographs, including several of me.

When I got home after my daytime cleaning shift, he was waiting for me. He was shaking and looked me straight in the face and said, just serving drinks, eh? and threw the photos at me and shouted, I will kill the bastard and stormed out of the house.

That was it, the next day I left Dorsey's. Tom started drinking and soon lost the taxi job, we then lost our home, our marriage was over, and it was all my fault. I move back in with my parents and Tom went to live with his widowed mother.

Around five weeks later the shock news that Mr Dorsey had been found murdered hit the news. The following week I learned that Tom had suddenly left the area.

(Dan)

You must make a formal statement here at the station Brenda, please give me your name and address, you have no alternative.

The phone went dead.

Billy had been spellbound and had even ignored his almost full whisky glass waiting by his side. He came out of his stare and downed a large swig. There certainly seems to be motive if this Brenda is telling the truth he thought, but why would she wait so long to come forward with this information.

Plenty to think about as he finished off his scotch.

CHAPTER 23

Billy got into the office early the next morning, but only just before Dan arrived, as he also had lots of questions running through his mind.

The two immediately started airing their thoughts: *"What I can't understand is why Brenda, if that is her real name, has only just decided to contact the Police, unless she is an out an out nutter"*, Billy said.

"Her story is far too detailed not to be true in my view Billy", Dan replied, *"and why is there no record of Brenda or any cleaner in Dorsey's records? she has claimed he paid her in cash and remember there was a considerable amount of cash found in Dorsey's safe according to the original investigation. I don't recall any record of any cleaners in his accounting books, do you, so maybe he did pay casual staff in cash".*

I'm glad you decided to record the phone call Danny boy, we've got to follow this up. We don't have her name, but we have got her mobile number, so we can get Boy Wonder to trace the subscriber details when he gets in", Billy said.

DC Sam Brown and Shivi arrived at the same time and were chatting together and laughing as they entered the office and settled at their desks. Dan and Billy looked at each other with a sort of satisfied smile.

"Shivi, play this audio recording" Billy said handing over the tape, *"you both need to hear this, and make a copy for the boss".*

All four sat in complete silence as they listened to the detailed descriptive telephone account from this lady cleaner calling herself Brenda.

"So, she immediately cut the call off as soon as you said she had to come in then Dan? Sam asked, "did you try to call back?"

Yep, I tried twice that same night and several times since, no reply", Dan said.

"Here's the mobile number Shivi, see what you can do with it while we let the boss listen to this recording" Billy said.

"Good timing lads", as they arrived at DI Morris's office, *"I was just about to call you, I've got some results back from the lab. The tooth* ***was*** *Dorsey's, it's been confirmed beyond doubt".* Mike announced.

"Did the postmark on the parcel give us any leads?", Billy asked.

"Not much, the parcel was really quite badly damaged, but from what little can be recovered it looks like it could have come from one of the London borough's" Mike replied.

"It seems the packaging, no more than a padded envelope, had been used before, and under forensic examination uncovered the remains of a partial address which they think was likely a recipient's address and that whoever received the original envelope had simply tried to eradicate the details and re-use the packaging, so the Polish and London connection is getting stronger. There were no clear prints on the outer packaging, which will have been handled several times in transit anyway, but the lab has recovered a good print on the piece of paper that the tooth was wrapped in, but there is no match in the system, ***and*** *we still don't have motive".*

Hearing the word motive, Dan and Billy looked at each other, then Billy passed the tape to Mike saying, *"You need to listen to this Boss".*

There was silence throughout the whole recording, with both old pals watching DI Morris's facial reactions at every stage.

As the tape ended, Mike said *"Well if this is genuine, we certainly have motive gents, you've got to find this lady and bring her in, if this turns out to be some kind of hoax, she will be charged with wasting Police time".*

"Shivi is working on her mobile phone number now, so hopefully we can identify her and bring her in" Billy said as they left DI Morris to go through the recording again alone.

On their way back downstairs, they saw Shivi walking quickly towards them. *"This Brenda has just rung in and wants to speak to Dan Nichols"* he said, *"hurry, I said you would get back to her straight away Dan".*

Back in the office Dan hurriedly called Brenda's mobile, and she answered immediately.

"Mr Nichols, I have to get this off my chest, I can't sleep at night, it's making me ill., I will talk to you again, can I see you today?".

"Yes, of course Brenda", Dan replied, and looking over at DC Sam Brown said, *"Would you feel more comfortable speaking to the female member of our team?"*.

After a short pause she said *"Yes, can she come to see me here today rather than at the Police Station?"*

"I'm sure Samantha would come and meet with you at your home Brenda" Dan said purposely looking to Sam for her approval, which he immediately got from her positive nod and thumbs up.

"Let me put you on to Sam now Brenda and you can make arrangements," and passed the phone to Sam.

After the briefest conversation with Sam scribbling down some notes she ended the call saying, *"I will be with you within the next half hour Brenda"*, while the others listened in silence.

"OK, I've got her address and will make my way over there now. Incidentally, she says her real name is Brenda, Brenda Barnes".

"We don't know this woman or anything about her Sam, you are not going on your own, Dan you go with her, you can take a back seat if she insists and will only speak to Sam alone, but at least you have spoken to her before, let's have her address and we can see if there is any background information on this Brenda Barnes or her husband Tom" Billy said.

As Dan and Sam were leaving, Billy added, *"Oh and see if there is anything whatsoever that may connect to a Polish link, no matter how small"*.

On their way to the address Dan said, *"why would someone wait all this time to come forward with what let's face it sounds like a convincing story?"*.

"We will hopefully find out the answer to that question today Dan", Sam replied.

"Just another thought Sam, Victor Collier's friend Krystna according to her old flatmate, had a job as a cleaner for a short period at the same time Collier was working for Dorsey, we need to locate this Krystna and Victor Collier as soon as possible" Dan said.

Back at the office Shivi carried out the usual background checks on

Brenda and Tom Barnes which covered Brenda's current address and previous addresses they had shared, with nothing of a detrimental nature known other than a few periods which showed they were in debt with a couple of County Court Judgments recorded.

"What do you think?" Dan said as the two drove back after meeting and taking a statement from Brenda Barnes.

"To be honest Dan, I felt a bit sorry for her, she is clearly riddled with guilt, whether it's justified or not, but at least we've got a clearer picture as to why it has taken her until now to come forward", Sam said.

They arrived back at the office just as Shivi and Billy were finishing for the day.

"The boss wants an update tomorrow on what more we've got" Billy said, *"so how did it go?"*

"Well, I've got to say it was interesting, and she does come across as a pretty honest witness", Sam said, as she passed Brenda Barnes signed statement to him.

"We can go through it all tomorrow" Billy replied as he grabbed his coat, and the team left for the day.

Outside Dan and Billy set off together as usual.

"Do you want me to fill you in over a quick beer at the C n A", Dan said.

"Can't tonight Danny boy, something I've got to do, see you in the morning" Billy replied giving his old pal a pat on the back as he headed of in a different direction.

Dan strolled off home thinking maybe Billy has got some planning to do for his usual DJ Compere stint at the Golden Ball open mike night on Friday, or maybe he is meeting up with Jenny. He was happy for Billy as his friendship with Jenny had blossomed, and it was Dan who had introduced her to him. Billy had tragically lost his wife due to cancer in the early part of their marriage whilst he was still serving in the army and the couple never had chance to even plan to have a family.

Now sat in the comfort of his own surroundings Dan was dwelling on what Brenda Barnes had told Sam earlier in his presence.

Out of the blue he thought of his old army Captain in London and remembering the brief time he worked for him at the private security and investigation firm the captain had set up on his retirement after Dan himself had also retired from the Military. The captain had been a vital contact after Dan had moved to Manchester to live what he thought at the time was going to be a relaxing comfortable retirement time. If only he had known.

He decided to send an email and update Captain on his new role with Billy and Mike Morris in this small newly set up Police cold case review team.

After going through the pleasantries, he gave a brief explanation how DI Mike Morris's retirement plan was cut short by immediately bringing him back in to head up a brand-new Police cold case review team at the Manchester station and how Billy and Dan himself had been recruited as part of the set-up then added:

You will remember Billy and Mike who you met at Mike's retirement party here a few months ago. We are working on something here where we are trying to locate a couple of possible witnesses who we believe may have moved from Manchester to the London area around ten years ago and wonder if I can throw a couple of names at you, just on the odd chance you may have come across them in any civil matters you have dealt with. Their names are not too common. Hope you don't mind, please let me know.

My best as ever.

Dan.

Before he even had chance to put the kettle on his laptop pinged, it was an instant reply.

Hi Dan

It doesn't surprise me that you and Billy are helping the local Constabulary AGAIN. Yep, throw the names over and I will see if we have anything on record.

Captain.

Reply

Brilliant, thanks. **Victor Collier** *and* ***Krystna Bartosz.***

Dan

CHAPTER 24

The following morning was taken up with discussing the details that Brenda Barnes had provided in her statement, which Billy had already read by now.

She had revealed further information which had embellished the information originally told to Dan during their recorded telephone conversation.

"So, she claims that her marriage to husband Tom was over after he found out what she was really doing at Dorsey's studio and shortly after this he left her, she then hears that he had left the area, she says even Tom's mother had no idea where he had disappeared to", Billy said reading over the statement.

"Yep, and by this time Tom's mother was sick with worry and her health deteriorated" Sam said.

"And in answer to the question we were all wondering about, why she has only now come forward with this information, she claims that around six months ago, out of the blue, she gets word that Tom had suffered a stroke and was in a hospital in the Birmingham area. She goes to visit him and sits by his bedside; Brenda tells him that she has had never forgiven herself for what her actions had made him do to Dorsey and that it had all been her fault.

She had held Tom's hand and although he couldn't speak at that time, he had smiled back at her and had tried to mouth, I am so sorry too.

Brenda had kept this news from his mother who by this time was herself quite ill", Dan said.

"But she says that was six months ago, why has she only come forward now, why not back then?" Shivi asked.

"Good question Shivi", Sam said, *"because a few weeks back she had word that Tom had suffered another stroke and had died, we have the death certificate.*

Tom's mother had also passed away by this time. Brenda says that she has lived all these years with the knowledge that her husband had committed murder, and all because of her. She still loved him and couldn't bear the thought of him going to prison, but now that both Tom and his mother were no longer here to suffer that pain, she knew she had to tell the truth even though she realised she would be charged with knowingly withholding the truth and even being an accomplice after the fact".

"I can see all that Sam, but where does the Polish connection come in?" Shivi said.

"Well, that's the thing, there doesn't appear to be one, when I introduced a brief question to see if Tom had any Polish friends, Brenda said she didn't know of any, apart from she thought a couple of the other taxi drivers where Tom had worked might have been Polish", Sam replied.

"Hang on, I'm just not getting this" Billy said, *"this woman is either a total fantasist, or what she is saying she believes is true, and she genuinely believes that her husband killed Dorsey, but apart from him saying he would kill him in a state of anger, he didn't exactly admit to it from his hospital bed, as he couldn't speak, there's absolutely no evidence".*

"I have to agree Billy, this doesn't gel with me, OK you could say there was motive and I suppose even opportunity as her husband had been to Dorsey's place before to pick up half cut supposed businessman in his taxi, but the anonymous parcel sent to the Police containing what we know IS Dorsey's tooth and note in an old Polish snuff box just doesn't connect with Brenda's story, no matter how much she believes it to be true", Dan said.

"I suppose we had better go and see what the boss thinks eh Dan?" Billy said as the two took Brenda Barnes statement upstairs to DI Morris's office.

On the way Billy couldn't resist,*" better see if we can spot Eve eh Dan, or even Paula maybe"* as he winked at Dan, *"I forgot to tell you, this Friday at the Golden Ball has been cancelled, so we had better let them know, don't want them turning up and being disappointed eh".*

After listening to Brenda Barnes statement Mike Morris agreed there was little in the way of evidence that Dorsey had been murdered by Tom Barnes, and unless other factors were forthcoming the team should press on with all other enquiries and get the original witnesses interviewed again.

Once out of the office Dan said, *"I didn't get chance to ask Billy, what was so important you couldn't meet up at the C n A the other night, was it to do with Friday nights Golden Ball cancellation?"*

"No, that's because they have had a really bad leak and the plumbers are in, looks like a fairly big job, no toilets even, but all will be OK for the next do".

"So, what **was** *so important then"* Dan said.

"Tell you later over a beer", Billy said with a wink and broad smile.

"OK team, let's push on with the other people we want to interview, get the names out again Shivi, and current addresses for those who gave their statements immediately after the murder, we need to interview them again". Billy said. Shivi and Sam nodded and got on with their work.

Later, settled in at the Crown & Anchor Dan said, *"Well come on Billy, what was so important the other night?".*

"Operation Toad in the Hole Danny Boy, get the beers in and I will tell you".

Now with Dan's complete attention Billy explained.

"Courtesy of little Maurice, AKA Honest John, and with a little bit of persuasion, I now had the name and address of the Toad, and a description. Maurice said he was a small slim fella who he said looks a bit like that Johnny Rotton, or was it Syd Snot, who was in a punk rock band years ago and said he only knew his first name was Terry.

I took Big Nigel from the Bull with me and waited in the car until we saw Terry leave his first floor Council flat and waited until he was alongside. I got out and said hello Terry, I've brought someone to meet you.

He said who the hell are you, then big Nigel got out of the car and stood towering next to him. I said this is Angus's brother, he's heard such a lot about you.

You should have seen his face Dan, his nervous eye twitch then transferred down to his shaking legs.

He said, no you've got the wrong person, I don't know anyone called Angus. I said yes you do, come on we'll remind you, and Nigel put him in the car and sat next to him on the back seat.

As we pulled up outside the railway arches, I said, there you see Terry, it's all coming back to you now isn't it.

With a bit of help from Nigel, he got out of the car, still visibly shaking.

I went to the back of the car and watched his face as I flipped the boot open. I can't imagine what he was thinking.

I leaned in and took out Angus's concertina, which I had cleaned and polished up and handed it to the Toad, who somehow didn't seem too slippery now as he clearly realised what all this was about.

I said now listen very carefully; we are going into the archway to see Angus. You are going to tell him that as you have enjoyed his playing and singing so much in the past, you decided to take his squeeze box and have it cleaned up for him as a gesture, got it?

He looked at me and then up at big Nigel and said nervously, will that be it then?

As we led him inside, I said, not quite, how much money have you got on you? He pulled his wallet out and said, here, you can have it. I looked and saw he had fifty quid. I gave him back the wallet and said, when you hand the concertina back to Angus, I also want you to give him your fifty quid as well, which will cover the money you stole from him when you took his concertina and the money he had his begging cup, and the 40 quid you got from Honest John, oh and a fiver towards the petrol for bringing you here.

Angus was sat in his old armchair inside the dimly lit corner by his sleeping area. As we approached him Polish Joe saw us and immediately came over to see what was happening. I nodded to him as he witnessed the Toad handing back the squeeze box and the 50 quid to the confused looking Angus, whilst quoting verbatim what I had instructed him to say.

Now surrounded by not only me and big Nigel, but also the large fearsome frame of Polish Joe, the still shaking Toad said, can I go now.

I smiled at Angus and Joe and led our pathetic arsehole of a human being back out to the car. He immediately said I'll go now; I got the message, then started to walk off. I said, no, we will give you a lift and drop you off a bit nearer home. He said no, it's OK I'll Walk.

Nigel helped him back into the car and we drove off.

Nobody said a word on the 10-minute journey back, and I kept looking in the rear mirror at our nervous passenger who was obviously wondering what was going to happen next, as he sat beside the expressionless faced giant of the man big Nigel. It was almost like a scene out of a Chicago mafia gangster movie.

I stopped the car in a dark unlit remote spot alongside the canal and leaned back looking the terrified Toad in the face. Makes you think, I said slowly, was it all worth it? I'm sure he thought the end is nigh, and he was going into the canal.

Let me tell you something I said, Old Angus lost his leg fighting in the forces, fighting for this country, this same country that now allows arseholes like you to live the way you do, stealing and drug dealing whilst no doubt living rent free on all the benefits and handouts you can fiddle, without ever doing an honest day's work in your life, now get out of my sight and **Foxtrot Oscar** *back to the shit hole you crawled out of.*

With that Nigel opening the back door and let him out.

I dropped Nigel at the Bull, as he was on bar duty that night and handed him a 20 quid note and thanked him, he had played his part perfectly and never spoke a word all night. He surprised me and said, put your money away, it was a pleasure to see some justice done and shook my hand".

"So, Operation Toad in the Hole is done and was a great success Billy, well done, I think you deserve a large scotch now", Dan said patting his old pal on the back.

"Nigel can certainly be deceiving then eh Billy," Dan said.

"He sure can Danny boy, do you know he was brought up in a care home until he was old enough to join the Grenadier Guards".

"What, Big Nigel joined the Grenadier Guards? Dan replied.

"No, but he was old enough" Billy said, and the two old pals burst out laughing.

CHAPTER 25

"This chap called Holroyd who got in touch as a result of the public appeal is coming in today, I can do the interview Billy" Sam said.

"You do that Sam, we've got the use of the main interview room, but before you see him, dig out the original statement given by the Holroyd fella who worked at the Council at the time of the murder, you never know, there may be some connection", Billy said.

Dan chipped in *"From memory Billy, I think Holroyd was actually a Councillor and had something to do with finances, I'll get the file for you Sam".*

Billy had noticed Shivi looking at his watch a couple of times. *"Fancy some coffee, I'll pop and get some"* Shivi said.

As he left Billy said, *"what's the betting he has arranged to be at the coffee machine at a set time to meet this Miranda girl".*

"Didn't know he had a girlfriend" Sam said, *"and she works here? I'll have to have a look at her then".*

When Shivi came back with the coffees, all three stared at him in silence.

"Well, was she on time?" Billy said.

"What, who" Shivi replied trying to look surprised. *"Miranda you turnip, we are not daft"* Billy said.

"Yeh, I did bump into her as it happens" Shivi replied trying to sound sort of matter of fact, as he put down the coffees and sat at his desk as quick as he could with his back towards the others.

Billy Dan and Sam all looked at each other and smiled.

Sam got the call that her Mr Holroyd was arriving to give his statement in an hour, so she left with her folder under her arm to take advantage of the quiet solitude of the interview room to go through Councillor Holroyd's old statement before her man arrived.

"She fits in well doesn't she" Dan said, *"and she is good at what she does I have to say, she certainly put Brenda Barnes at ease when we went to see*

her the other day".

"Yep, Mike Morris said she was highly regarded and could well be on her way up the ranks before too long" Billy replied.

The phone rang and Shivi answered, *"Billy there's a chap called Nigel wants to speak to you".*

Billy took the call and after listening in silence said, *"OK, I'll see you tonight".*

"What was all that about" Dan asked. *"I said we would call in at the Bull tonight, and I can see him then Dan."*

"What do you mean WE will call in the Bull?"

"Come on Danny boy, it is Friday, and I did get a message to Eve the other day to say tonight's Golden Ball gig was cancelled and promised we would probably call in the Bull instead to say hello to the girls. You still got that clean shirt ironed haven't you Dan?"

"Good of you to mention it to me Billy" Dan said shaking his head, *"what time then?"*

They arrived at the Bull just after 7.30 and the place was already busy with mostly the usual faces, including the reporter Headline Eddie who when he spotted Billy, quickly turned away avoiding eye contact.

"Go and see if you can spot the ladies Dan, while I get the drinks in and see big Nigel" Billy said.

Dan couldn't see any sign of Eve or Paula anywhere and was just about to join Billy at the bar when he heard a voice say hello Dan. When he turned, it was Paula who had just arrived.

"Have you seen Eve; I am a bit late, and she is always early, a creature of habit you might say". I think we got that message loud and clear last time Dan thought to himself.

"No, I've just been looking while Billy was at the bar, but I've not seen her, shall we sit at this table here, we should be able to spot her coming in from here", Dan replied. *"You sit down Paula, and I will catch Billy at the bar and get you a drink, G n T was it?".*

Billy was in conversation with Nigel when he arrived and Dan just caught the end of the conversation, which sounded a bit serious.

"Sorry to interrupt, but can you add a Gin and Tonic to those drinks Billy, Paula is sat over there".

Walking back with the drinks Dan said, *"You seemed to be in deep conversation with Nigel, he wasn't offering to knit you a cardigan, was he?".*

"Tell you later Dan", he whispered, *"Well Paula, how lovely to see you"* Billy said, automatically going into charm mode.

With no sign of Eve, at least it gave the three of them the opportunity to share some uninterrupted conversation.

"Have you settled in a bit now Paula, it must seem a bit strange coming back up North after so long." Dan said., *"I know it took me quite a while after being away for most of my working life, so I know what it can be like".*

"I think I will feel much better when I move, I rented a place that Eve recommended just until I found a place of my own Dan".

"Having any luck on that score?" Billy said.

"Not really, but I keep looking and I'm sure I'll find something suitable", Paula replied.

After half an hour of quite pleasant relaxed general chit chat, Paula's mobile rang, it was Eve. *"She's had to cancel"* Paula said, *"something about an urgent meeting for one of her many local neighbourhood committees which she is chair of, and she says they can't do without her".*

Dan and Billy looked at each other clearly thinking, why doesn't that surprise us.

Dan was beginning to enjoy the relaxed atmosphere and easy chatting when Billy said, *"Oh there's someone over there I want to see, excuse me for a minute".*

"You go ahead; I'll get some drinks in" Dan said as Billy got up and wandered off.

"What about you Paula, another G n T, I think I'm going to have a nice relaxing glass of red wine", Dan said suddenly feeling comfortable in Paula's company even more so without Billy chipping in, *"It is Friday*

after all and I'm sure we have all had a busy week".

"You know Dan, I think I would quite enjoy a glass of wine as well, do you mind" she said.

"My pleasure Paula" Dan replied, feeling quite pleased with himself and getting the impression that Paula was also feeling more comfortable without Eve's dominant presence.

On his way to the bar, he saw Billy talking to the newspaper reporter Billy refers to as Headline Eddie. Wonder what that's all about he thought in view of Billy's previous remarks about Eddie Frost.

Dan arrived back with a bottle of Pinot Noir in one hand and three glasses in the other. *"Decided to get a bottle, I know Billy also enjoys an odd glass of vino".*

With all three enjoying the wine, the remainder of the evening went quickly with Billy's entertaining chat relaxing the conversation even more.

Paula eventually said, *"I think I should be getting off now, but I have really enjoyed tonight, thank you".*

Dan looked at his watch and said, *"How are you getting home Paula?",*

"Well, I normally walk back with Eve as it's only 10 minutes away for both of us, just the other side of the Police Station, but I'll probably just get a taxi".

"No", Dan said, *"we have to go that way ourselves, so we can walk together can't we Billy",*

"Of course, Paula, it will be our pleasure". Billy agreed.

After escorting Paula home Dan said, *"Fancy a nightcap at the Crown and Anchor? then you might tell me what all this business with big Nigel and Eddie Frost was about in the Bull earlier".*

"I get the impression you have taken a bit of a shine to Paula Danny Boy, eh?".

"Don't changed the subject Billy, but I suppose I do quite like Paula, she is very easy to be with isn't she".

The C n A was as quiet as usual, so no problem getting a table in the corner.

"Now come on then, what was all that about in the Bull tonight, Billy?"

"OK, when we went to see Angus the other night, I told you that Polish Joe came over to see what we were up to, well apparently Nigel said he saw the big Pole sniffing some powder from the back of his hand as he approached us and never thought anything about it until afterwards.

He said he thought it was a bit strange that we were there to teach this young fella the error of his ways as a thief and drug addict, when drugs were being used by the supposed friend of Angus inside the arcade.

I told Nigel I hadn't noticed that, and I was surprised, as so far as I knew there had never been any evidence of drug taking, in fact just the opposite, as I knew Angus was very anti-drugs and I got the impression Polish Joe shared that same view".

"What do you think then?" Dan asked.

"I'm going to pop back to the railway arches tomorrow Dan and see for myself".

"And what was the chat with Eddie Frost about tonight? I thought you couldn't stand the man, and he didn't seem too pleased to see you when we first arrived".

"Ah, if you remember, when I saw him at Piccadilly Station and he knew I had figured out what he was up to, I told him if I had any snippets of info which he might want to work on as an expose article, I would let him know. Well, I gave him details of the Toad, where he lives, what he looks like and what he gets up to and suggested if he gets a few of his people from the paper to keep an eye on this young fella's activities, he could well get the credit for exposing the little turd and maybe an exclusive".

"Do you think he will go for it Billy?"

"Well, even if it doesn't come off, at least the Toad will spot that he is being watched and it might give him a few sleepless nights not knowing if it could be Police surveillance or some other local villains watching him".

The weekend turned out to be quite relaxing for Dan, spending a pleasant time at home.

After a nice morning stroll, including a now regular walk to the canal area where Owen's lifeless body had been discovered by an inquisitive boxer dog and called in to the Police by the boxer's owner Mr Hudson.

In the solitude of his walk, he was thinking about natures sometimes unfairness, why somebody like Owen can be born with severe learning difficulties plus autism, with the mental capability of just a young child and living with all these disadvantages throughout his life into his adulthood, when somebody like this fella the Toad can live a perfectly normal life. Where is the fairness in that.

His mind was never too far away from the Dorsey case and wondered how Sam's interview with this Holroyd chap went.

Dan couldn't help thinking back to the events which lead to Billy being approached to be part of the new cold case Police review team to be headed up by DI Mike Morris.

After the aging duo's sometimes unorthodox but vital evidence gathering in the earlier matter of Dan's neighbour Kevin Carter had successfully led to Carter being convicted and jailed along with his co-conspirators as part of an elaborate animal charity scam, Dan and Billy were praised by the local Constabulary.

The information they also uncovered in the mystery of Owen's stolen dog, and then poor Owen's subsequent questionable death by the canal side, further highlighted their potential usefulness to the understaffed local Police Force.

Billy had agreed to come out of retirement and accept the cold case position, but only on condition that Dan himself was also accepted as part of the team, hence the old pal's now daily evidence gathering investigation and research work from their tiny cold case review team office at the Police Station.

Now back in his apartment Dan made himself a sandwich and poured himself a glass of Pinot Noir, his very favourite red wine.

How nice that Paula had also wanted to share a glass with him the other night at the Bull. He thought about the fact that they both had something in common, returning to Manchester after such a long time away, and then remembering that Eve had said Paula's late husband was in the military, so maybe they had even more in common.

Yes, Dan did quite like Paula, and he made his mind up that it would be nice if he could see her again.

CHAPTER 26

"*So, let's have a look at the statement from your Mr Holroyd then Sam"* Billy said as the team gathered for their first morning meet.

"Well, it sure was interesting" Sam replied, *"the earlier suggestion that there may even be some connection with the Councillor Holroyd was spot on, listen to this, Councillor Frederick J Holroyd is the father of Jonathan Holroyd who I interviewed on Friday, well I say is the father, I mean* **was** *his father, as Councillor Holroyd passed away a couple of months ago.*

Jonathan comes across as a very bright straight forward man, who says he qualified here in Manchester as an accountant and now lives and works in Canada for a huge PLC group as part of their financial team and has done so for the past six years. He is a married man living comfortably in Toronto with his Canadian born wife and two young children".

"So if he still lives in Canada, why is he here and why has he responded to the public appeal about the Dorsey murder a decade ago?" Billy said.

"After his father died, Jonathan said he was contacted by his father's lawyers who were acting as executors, and it had taken them a while to track Jonathan down, as no other living relatives could be traced", Sam continued.

"Jonathan's mother had died some years earlier and his dad had lived alone. Jonathan had inherited his parents modest house, and he had the job of clearing out the property before it was to be put on the market".

"But what has that got to do with the Dorsey case?" Billy said.

"Let Sam finish for goodness' sake Billy", Dan said.

"When going through the house Jonathan came across a small bureau which was locked. When he managed to get it open, he found a laptop and several folders containing paperwork, some of which were exchanges with Mr Dorsey the photographer. He was aware that his father's Council department had always used Dorsey to photograph and film the Council's formal events etc. so that was no surprise, but what he found on the laptop he didn't understand.

There were old emails to and from a man called Zac Gold. These emails indicated that when attending seminars in London specifically for finance leaders in different government departments, his father had become friends with one of the other regular attendees a man just referred to as Peter, who worked in a finance department at one of the government departments based in London. The seminars compared and shared systems used in different areas to achieve maximum efficiency.

This friend Peter had talked about this man Zac Gold who he said was a wealthy investment broker who he, Peter had personally made good profits dealing with and had promised to put Zac in touch with Councillor Holroyd although they had never actually met, as apparently Zac Gold operated mainly out of the country.

Some later dated emails included three-way communications which included his father, Zac Gold ***and*** *Arnold Dorsey and were on first name terms. They were discussing a potential investment in a company registered overseas and the figures mentioned were very substantial.*

This all seemed strange to Jonathan and sort of out of character for his father, plus the fact that his father had virtually no savings in his only bank account which also seemed strange. It was at that point that he felt he should pass this stuff on to the Police in response to the public appeal just in case the Dorsey connection may be significant".

"That all sounds a bit dodgy" Dan said. "Was there any mention of who this overseas company was on the laptop Sam".

"Jonathan said there were some files on the laptop that he couldn't open and that was another reason for passing this on, he said this could even have the hall marks of a classic scam, almost like a long firm fraud where small sums are invested in the first place which quickly doubled their return, giving the greedy investor confidence.

He then explained that this type of scam, is where the broker says he has sure fire insider information offering huge no risk returns on large investments, then once the large amounts are sent, the supposed expert dealer disappears." Sam replied.

"Shivi, you see what else you can find on the laptop while Dan you go through the paper folders, Billy said, *"I'm going to pop up and tell the boss about this".*

"What about my witness Jonathan Holroyd", Sam said, *"he is due to fly back to Canada at the weekend".*

"I'm pretty sure the boss will say we will need to speak to him again Sam, so tell him to make himself available, at least that gives us time before the weekend". Billy said.

Before going through this latest paperwork Dan decided to go over the old witness statements again in particular the very brief statement Councillor Holroyd had given at the time. He also looked at his own notes where he had spotted and purposely highlighted the similar, and in some cases exact wording a few of the other people from the Council Offices had used in their statements.

Most of these witnesses claimed that they only knew Dorsey from a business viewpoint and didn't know him personally and had never even visited his studio building. Strange then that Councillor Holroyd also made this same claim, when it now seems he and Dorsey were in fact in some kind of investment business together.

Mike Morris listened intently as Billy explained this latest information obtained from Jonathan Holroyd. He remained unusually quiet for a second or two before saying: *"Was there any mention who this friend Peter was, and which government department in London where he worked".*

"Now you mention it, no I don't think there was, but Shivi is going to see what else he can find on the laptop" Billy replied.

"Well, you get off now", DI Morris said cutting the conversation dead.

That was a bit odd Billy thought as he made their way back downstairs.

He had only been back in the office a matter around twenty minutes when the phone rang and Shivi said, *"it's DI Morris for you Billy, he wants you to go back to his office now and take all the Holroyd stuff, the laptop and folder with the papers with you".*

Billy and Dan looked at each other in surprise and without saying a word Billy grabbed the laptop and papers and made his way back upstairs.

When he arrived, DCI Gill was in the office with Mike Morris who said, *"Take a seat Billy".*

With a confused look on his face Billy sat down wondering why the hell the DCI was there.

"We know you always had a bit of a cavalier streak in you Billy and sometimes feel convention gets in the way of dealing with things, but on this occasion, I had no alternative other than to involve the Chief Inspector", Mike continued.

Billy thought he was in for some kind of telling-off at the least, immediately thinking that his private unofficial dealing with the Toad had somehow got back to the ears of his superiors. Probably that devious smart arse reporter Eddie Frost trying to get one over on him he guessed.

"What do you know about the name Zac Gold Billy?" DCI Geoff Gill said.

"Other than that name appearing in these messages absolutely nothing yet, we've not had chance to do that research". Billy answered.

"Well don't do that research", the DCI said.

"What, how can we try to get to the bottom of who and why Dorsey was murdered if we can't include every single piece of information we receive" Billy said.

Mike Morris raised his eyebrows, shook his head then turned to DCI Gill and said, *"I knew this tact wouldn't work, I think we had better just explain".*

"Explain what boss?" Billy said looking puzzled.

"OK, what I am going to tell you, you must keep to yourself, and not discuss with anybody, not even the other members of your team, and that is an order, understood?" DCI Gill said. *"Now just sit there and listen"*, he continued pointing a headmaster type finger at Billy.

"Several years ago, the Met had a purge on the drug smuggling gangs where a secret team of undercover officers infiltrated the gangs over a long period of time which led to successful raids and seizures of drugs, and large amounts of drug money in cash. The operation was so secret that only a tiny handful of senior officers were aware of the set up.

The large amounts of cash seized was then used by the undercover guys to buy drugs and thereby gather intelligence to identify the main players, which led to arrests and convictions and of course more seizures of drugs and cash, and so this successful operation continued.

The cash was handled by a secret accounts department within Scotland Yard which again was known only to the few senior officers. This under the radar accounts department was run by just three men who monitored and distributed the cash for the undercover guys to carry out their work.

Over a period, one of the long serving accountants retired. Shortly afterwards a second was diagnosed with a terminal illness and very soon died. This left just one man with complete unaccountable control over the whole system until the other positions could be filled.

It transpired that temptation was just too much for this lone accountant who over a fairly short period managed to embezzle the huge amount of an estimated £5 million, most of which we only later discovered he had transferred to an offshore bank account using false details.

When his crime was discovered, the accountant Peter was arrested, admitted the theft and disclosed that he had purchased a holiday home in Marbella in his wife's name, and accepted a deal to plead guilty and serve a five-year custodial sentence".

Billy sat quietly throughout, but just couldn't resist any longer and said, *"But what's all this old Scotland Yard stuff got to do with us and our case Chief?".*

"If you let me finish, I will tell you" The DCI said beginning to lose his patience.

"Of the estimated millions embezzled only £1.2 million was recovered from the seizure of the luxury holiday home in Marbella under the Proceeds of Crime Act., the remaining amount has never been located".

"Well, who was this bent Met accountant Peter then, and why have we never heard about this before", Billy continued to interrupt.

Mike Morris jumped in fearing DCI Gill was going to explode.

"Billy this mess within the Met was bad enough, do you think they were going to advertise the cock up? There was no need for any publicity as he pleaded guilty, you can imagine what the national press would have made

of it, plus more importantly there were still undercover officers out there, and still are, whose lives would have been put at risk".

When we got this latest information from you which included the name of a Zac Gold, that's when we had to step in and explain. His name had been flagged up to just senior officers in all forces.

The Met always felt that Zac Gold was probably the false name our bent Met accountant Peter used to salt away most of the stolen money overseas, although he always denied that and insisted Zac Gold did exist but admitted he had never actually met him.

This is the first time this name has come up in any Police investigation, so now that we appear to have the possibility of a remote lead as to exactly where the money could be, and eventually try to recover it, this will need to be handled by a specialist team and more than likely be a long drawn out job, so we want you to forget this aspect going forward.

If information comes to light which has any bearing at all on the Dorsey case you will be informed in due course, but until then concentrate on the other leads you have, and remember, no word of this to anyone, understood? now leave this laptop and folder with me".

"What makes you think this bent now ex-convict Peter is suddenly going to tell you where you can get your hands on the rest of the stolen money now, when he has kept it hidden all these years, I bet he has even buggered off abroad and living a life of luxury after doing his time, probably reduced for good behaviour no doubt" Billy said.

Mike Morris was also now running out of patience and said *"Billy, the thieving accounted didn't even serve his five-year sentence, he died of a heart attack in prison after only 20 months, so nobody will be talking to him".*

"Well, I'm glad there has been some sort of justice then" Billy said.

DI Morris looked to DCI Gill who opened the office door, nodded at Billy to go without saying another word.

CHAPTER 27

"*What was all that about*" Dan said when Billy eventually arrived back at the office. He had been desperately thinking of how he would answer that question he knew he was going to face from Dan and the others all the way down from DI Morris's office.

"With all this overseas company business stuff and Shivi having to spend valuable time trying to get into probably locked folders on the laptop, and with me having the laptop with me, I asked the boss why that job couldn't be dealt with by the expert IT staff normally used to sort these things out and let us get on with the job in hand.

After a while I finally persuaded him to do that, as long any intelligence that comes to light that has any bearing of our case, we will be kept in the loop", Billy said.

"I suppose that will lighten our load Billy" Dan said.

"So, Sam, you can tell your witness Jonathan Holroyd we don't need to speak to him again, the boss now has the file with all his contact details. If anything comes to light that may have any bearing on the Dorsey case, we will be informed. Trying to persuade DI Morris wasn't easy ", Billy continued, trying to avoid direct eye contact with the others,

"Now let's go over what we have got, i.e. the Polish connection and the mystery tooth package etc. and also the theory presented by Brenda Barnes that her dead husband murdered Dorsey, who knows, he could have hired a Polish hitman".

When Dan arrived home, he noticed the *To Let* sign for Carter's old ground floor flat was still on display. He couldn't help reflecting on how he and Billy had exposed Kevin Carter and his old university student colleague's animal charity scam, and how they had conned thousands of pounds from vulnerable pensioners. The two old pals cunning joint evidence gathering had finally resulted in Carter and his gang of thieves being arrested, convicted and jailed.

After pondering the day's events, he checked his computer and saw an email had come in from Captain in London.

"Hi Dan

I've picked up some information re the Polish sounding lady Krystna Bartosz.

Give me a call when you are free".

Captain.

Dan couldn't wait and rang straight away. It seemed quite a while before Captain answered.

"Hi Dan, sorry, I am out and about, I will email what we've got later tonight, must ring off now".

Obviously out on a job Dan thought, *"Thanks Captain".*

The information that finally came through by email certainly sounded promising. During some routine civil matters Captain was able to confirm that he had an address in the Greater London area where the name of Krystna Bartosz had appeared.

He stressed that he had not had her address confirmed as the information was from a while ago and didn't know how serious Dan's Police interest in the name was and didn't want to spook her just in case it may prompt her to disappear. You will have to pay the address a visit yourself Dan he had said.

Dan couldn't wait until the next morning and rang Billy straight away.

"Billy, we've got a lead on Krystna Bartosz in the London area from the captain".

"Just in the middle of something Dan, will call you back".

Wonder what he's up to at this time of night Dan thought looking at his watch.

It was a good 30 minutes before Billy rang back. *"What have we got from London then Dan?"*

Dan explained what Captain had found, *"At least we've got some positive intelligence to work on now eh Billy, I still think the way they both acted after Dorsey's murder suggests they knew more than they ever said"* Dan continued. *"Anyway, what have you been up to at this time of night Billy?"*

"I've been to the railway arches to have a word with Polish Joe, will explain

in the morning Dan, we may even have more to report to the boss".

Wonder what he meant by that Dan thought as he turned in for the night.

The next morning, with no other leads, Sam and Shivi had started digging further into Brenda Barnes claim that her husband Tom killed Dorsey in a rage of anger after finding out what he had persuaded Brenda to do at the studio in the evenings.

"Go and see Brenda Barnes again Sam and see if you can get any DNA or even prints from anything she still has of her late husband, and Shivi, you see what you can find about Tom Barnes after he left Manchester, where he lived, where he worked, anything, he may have confided in someone about his past, who knows, he could have hired a Polish hit man. Statistics apparently show that the motive for most murders are money, revenge or love". Billy said.

During a brief lunch break Billy said, *"Do you remember big Nigel telling me he thought he saw Polish Joe sniffing drugs, well I paid a visit to the railway arches last night to have a word. It turned out that Joe, whose full name is Josef Horovitz, was sniffing snuff, not drugs, he just laughed and pulled a small snuff box out of his pocket to show me, he said he was proud that he had inherited it from his father, and he believed it was his grandfathers before that".*

"Well, I suppose that makes sense eh, Sam did tell us that the staff at the Polish restaurant she worked at were snuff takers", Dan said.

"Yeh, but listen to this, the tin looked very similar to the one received anonymously at the station from what I can remember Dan, I need to have another look at that photograph we have of the package and snuff tin".

"You're not suggesting that Polish Joe has anything to do with this are you Billy".

"No, not at all, the information about the package has never been made public, but the Polish here are a very close-knit community, and I just wonder if the boss might agree to let us show the photograph to Joe to see if there is any reaction, what do you think Dan".

After a minute's thought Dan said, *"I've got a better idea Billy, why don't you tell Joe that I am a bit of a history buff, particularly with Polish artefacts such as snuff boxes etc. and I have lots of photographs of examples and would be really interested to see if his is amongst them. We could get Shivi to download a few other photo examples and slip our one in amongst them to see if he reacts".*

"That's actually not a bad idea Sherlock, but I still think it will be best to run it past Mike first, I'll pop up and have a word with him", Billy said.

"Oh, and at the same time tell him we now have these new leads in London, the Captain has suggested that we go down there and see if we can follow up the info and speak to Bartosz" Dan said.

"Will do Danny boy, I'll go up and see if he is free now".

"Well, you do seem to have this persuasive influence over Mike don't you Billy", Dan quipped.

Billy didn't respond, just kept his head down and couldn't look at Dan as he left.

On his way upstairs he couldn't help reflecting on his last meeting in Mike's office and was hoping the Chief Inspecter wasn't there today, but his thoughts were interrupted by Paula who was just coming out of the office into the corridor and stopped to say a brief hello. Billy was quite glad of the distraction, and they exchanged niceties with Billy asking about Eve.

As they parted and continued their separate ways, Paula turned back and asked how Dan was and said to pass on her "hello". He sensed there could be some kind of attraction going on here between Paula and his old pal and was smiling to himself as he entered DI Morris's office.

"What are you looking so pleased about". Mike said.

"Just a progress update boss, we think we have a lead on where we might find the Polish lady Bartosz. You remember meeting Dan's old boss in the army, he still just calls him Captain who has a security and investigation company in London, well The Captain came up with an address in the London area where we will find her. We would like to go down there and see what we can find, what do you think?" Billy said.

"It doesn't take two of you to do that" Mike replied sharply, *"Let Dan do*

it, you have plenty to do up here, I've got a meeting to go to Billy".

DI Morris clearly wasn't in the best of moods, so Billy decided best not to even mention the Polish Joe snuff tin idea.

Dan had been going through the old statements of the others who had worked at the Council Office alongside Counsellor Holroyd. He noticed that two had worked in the same Department of Finance with Holroyd.

He gave the statements to DC Sam Brown. *"Sam, have a look through these please, get Shivi to update their details, whether they still work at the Council, their addresses etc. anything you can find, we need to speak to them again, they may just know something about Counsellor Holroyd, or should I say the late Counsellor Holroyd".*

"I was going to suggest that Dan now that I have no need to speak to Jonathan the Holroyd son", Sam replied.

"Oh, and Shivi, do me good copy of the snuff tin which arrived in the mystery package, I may need it". Dan said just as Billy arrived back.

"How did it go upstairs?" Dan said.

"I think the boss is under a bit of pressure from the powers above to start getting some results now that the public are aware of the Dorsey murder re-investigation, and of course the local press is constantly on his back. I think it's best if you go and check out this possible lead on your own Dan, while I push on with what we've got here".

"OK, I'll do that straight away, no problem. What about the Polish Joe idea. Did he go for that?"

"Just leave that with me Danny boy" Billy replied.

CHAPTER 28

The rain was bouncing down as the 8.20am train to London Euston left Piccadilly Station spot on time. Good to be back in good old Manchester Dan thought to himself as he looked out of the carriage window with a wry smile on his face.

The journey was pleasant enough, not too busy and surprisingly quiet with most seated around him listening through earphones and subconsciously nodding away presumably to their favourite music, whilst others were typing away on their laptops.

Arrival at Euston was only 20 minutes late after a delay at Birmingham New Street. The onward trip by tube to Chancery Lane was as expected like joining a tribe of "worker ants", with numbers increasing at every station stop in between, making it impossible to grab the odd vacated seating spot, let alone make your standing position any more comfortable.

It had been his Commanding Officer in the Intelligence Corp who he still calls Captain to this day who had educated Dan that worker ants are all female, whereas *"soldier ants"* are slightly larger and all male species. Captain was full of little facts like that, a reminder to pay attention to every tiny detail Dan guessed.

In contrast to Manchester the weather was dry and sunny, and the short walk from the tube station to the office brought back many memories. Dan had rented a small flat situated just a stroll from the office.

The office itself was located discreetly tucked away in a minor back street, but conveniently close to some of the high-profile law firms in the surrounding area, many of which provided Captain's company with regular work ranging from insurance claim investigation, locating missing debtors, even criminal defence work and just about everything in between.

Captain welcomed Dan with a firm handshake and the two chatted as they entered one of the small offices. After a brief catch up, they were joined by Tim Symonds who Dan had not met before, but Captain had spoken highly of his manager who had joined the company after a long military career just after Dan himself had left and moved to Manchester. Tim spoke several languages Captain explained, adding that operating in London, it was a skill that was a great advantage and often called upon.

Dan's brief spell working in London had served as a gradual transition to civilian life after his whole adult career in the military, having joined up as a teenager on the same day as his schoolboy friend Billy.

It still seemed strange that the two old pals were now working together as part of the new cold case review team from a small office in the same Manchester Police station where Billy had worked as PC Oliver after his own spell in the army.

"I'm going to leave you with Tim, he has the information on the name you are interested in", Captain said. *"We can chat later".*

Tim had a folder with him and explained how they had come across the name of Bartosz. It had been a simple accident injury claim, and the insurance company client wanted a statement taking from Krystna Bartosz amongst others who had apparently witnessed the accident on a supermarket car park where a shopper had been quite seriously injured by a reversing car, which failed to stop even after the impact.

Tim had been tasked with this job as he spoke some Polish, assuming it may be necessary, although he said in the event the lady spoke perfect English.

For a someone who spoke multiple languages Tim was a surprisingly quiet man of few words, who spoke only when pointing out what was in the folder. Dan had tried to engage in lighter matters, asking Tim how many languages he spoke, only to get the answer, *he couldn't remember.*

This job had taken place a couple of months ago. Dan asked if he could remember whether there had been a male person present when he had first interviewed Krystna, and he said there wasn't, or at least he hadn't seen one. He also asked if he knew whether the lady had a daughter, but Tim said he didn't know.

After getting directions to the address, Dan thanked Tim and was able to have another brief word with Captain before deciding how best to approach his task.

It came as no surprise when Captain said that Tim would drive Dan to the address and assist if he could. He also told Dan that he had done a quick search on the address which showed that the name of a Marek Bartosz was also listed there with Krystna Bartosz, who he assumed to be her husband.

So was this all just a coincidence, the Krystna Bartosz they were interested in was just a young lady at the relevant time in Manchester and was certainly not married, Bartosz was her maiden name, which is a reasonably common Polish surname, so this may not be the same person. Dan had to think how best to approach this as he was being driven to the address.

Tim explained that the journey to the address would take around half an hour. Dan was pleased that there was little if any conversation during this time and was thankful that Tim was indeed a man of few words, as this allowed him to think of the best approach and read again through the statement Krystna Bartosz had given.

Just before they reached the location, Dan put his idea to Tim, who said nothing, just nodded in agreement.

The door was answered by an adult male. Tim apologised for calling unannounced and asked if it was convenient to speak to Krystna, simply to clarify a couple of small points on her statement re the incident on the supermarket car park

The chap looked a little puzzled as if he was wondering why this should take two men and nervously, with sort of a delayed intake of breath, asked for some ID to be produced. Tim had anticipated this, showed his ID and quickly said that Dan was a colleague from the office who witnesses may have to meet later just in case the matter has to go to court and any of the witnesses were called to give evidence, although he stressed that this was highly unlikely in this case.

The two were taken into a small lounge where Krystna Bartosz was sitting on a settee reading. Tim again explained why they were calling and took the statement out of the folder and said he just wanted to be clear on a couple of details. At this point the man who it was assumed was Marek Bartosz came and sat beside the lady in a sort of supportive or even protective way.

Tim then demonstrated why Captain highly rated him as he took over completely asking questions to clarify in just a little more precise detail as to exactly where she had been standing when she witnessed the car reversing into the accident victim, and could she remember who it was who called for an ambulance and was she one of the shoppers in the car park who had gone to help the injured person and had given the Police a description of the car and the driver.

During this time whilst Tim was appearing to write the answers in the folder, Dan was left to quietly observe as much as he could about Mr Bartosz and the surroundings of the room.

The whole thing took no more than about fifteen minutes, during which time Mr Bartosz never spoke. Tim thanked both Mr and Mrs Bartosz and as he and Dan were being shown from the room, Dan who also hadn't spoken up to this moment pointed to a framed photograph standing on top of a small free standing well stocked bookcase. The photograph was of a young girl appearing to be dressed in a school uniform and Dan politely asked if this was their daughter, to which Krystna Bartosz responded by rather proudly saying yes, this is Hanna, she is now almost sixteen and studying art at college.

At the door Dan reached out to Mr Bartosz to shake hands to add his thanks.

On the drive back Dan told Tim that he was really impressed at the way he had dealt with the situation so convincingly after only just being made aware of Dan's objective.

Feeling that his day's objective had been accomplished, Dan again said his thanks to Captain for his help, and praised Tim for the calm and convincing way in which he played his part.

They shook hands, with Captain telling Dan that if any information regarding a person by the name Victor Collier came to light during any future job, he would contact Dan immediately. Dan had kept his observations to himself and was conscious of not saying too much but ended by saying that today's help may prove to be sufficient.

On the train back to Manchester Dan used the time to reflect on his time in the Bartosz home and make his observation notes. He then carried out some online research.

Whilst Tim had been asking his well thought out questions, Dan had noticed that Mr Bartosz was wearing what looked like a gold signet ring on his right hand which appeared to have something engraved on it. Dan had purposely shaken hands with him on his way out of the house to get a close look at the ring and he was pretty sure that it displayed the initials **VC**.

This together with the photograph of the daughter aged almost sixteen called Hanna, and the bookshelf with book covers showing Historical Art subjects had convinced Dan that Marek Bartosz is Victor Collier. He had also noticed that when the chap had answered the door, he appeared to have a very slight stammer.

Captain's words, *"always pay attention to the small details"* forever embedded in his mind.

He couldn't wait to tell Billy.

By the time he got home it was mid evening and Dan reflected on his day in London and suddenly began to realise that he was no longer a young man and including the travel it had been quite a tiring day.

CHAPTER 29

Sam Brown and Shivi were already at their desks when Dan arrived followed within minutes by Billy who greeted the team with a broad smile and a cheery "good morning", clearly in an upbeat mood.

"How did your London trip go then Dan" Billy said.

"Never mind that, what have you been up to, to put that smile on your face" Dan replied.

"I spent most of yesterday on this Polish snuff box plan and then in the evening had a nice catch up with Jenny, it was her birthday, and we went out for a nice meal".

"Who is Jenny" Sam said.

"Billy's lady friend, I introduced Jenny to him quite a while back now, she is really nice", Dan said, remembering back to how he first met Jenny when she was his neighbour Owen's carer. The memory of that awful time when Owen's body was found at the canal still made him shudder.

The investigations that he and Billy made at the time surrounding Owen's death still convinced them even now that Owen was murdered, and it was no accident. They had passed all their findings to the local Police and that case was now in the hands of a Homicide Team from another Force and they are still awaiting the outcome. Dan was still in that reflective mode when Billy suddenly said.

"Listen to this, did you know that Poland once had a monarchy? Back in the late 17 hundreds in Warsaw, King Stanislaus Augustus was said to have had a metal snuff box with a royal crest engraved on it. Even the aristocracy soon had their own family crest engraved snuff boxes, it was quite common to have a family heirloom inside the box, a cutting of their child's hair for instance or other keepsakes.

In the early 1950's after the end of WW2, Poland had its own criminal Mafia type gangs, sort of the Krays type activity, protection and other stuff. They had their own version of their snuff boxes in which they could send a message to people who owed them money or had double crossed them, but inside would likely be the remains of a cut off finger or ear, and sometimes even more intimate parts of their criminal enemy's anatomy as a warning to others. What do you think of that?"

The others sat open mouthed in surprised silence.

Dan finally said, *"Have you been watching University Challenge again".*

Billy laughed and said, *"I spent quite a bit of time yesterday with Polish Joe, he is actually a very intelligent fella who has a degree in history, particularly in Polish history. Had he not fallen on hard times after his time in the military he was planning to try to get into the teaching profession, but things didn't work out for him".*

"Did you take photographs of the different snuff boxes to show him" Dan asked.

"Yep, I did Dan, Shivi had pulled some sample shots from various websites and then included the copy of our exhibit".

"And was there any reaction when it came to him seeing our one" Dan asked.

"He did say he recognised all the sample shots, but I guess that isn't surprising as we know they are visible on the various websites, but he admitted he hadn't seen our one before, and he really studied the engraved pattern for quite some time, it appeared to puzzle him.

At least it was interesting to learn about the Polish criminal gangs and how they used their snuff boxes to send a warning to anyone who double crossed them. A good job we only got Dorsey's tooth, and the murderer stopped at only ***kicking*** *him in the orchestra stalls".* Billy said. *"Now come on, what about your London trip Dan".*

Dan now took centre stage whilst the other three listened. He talked through his meeting with Captain and his new manager Tim Symonds, who had played his role so well to enable Dan to gather the surprising information whilst they were in the Bartosz home.

"Isn't it normal for the bride to take the groom's surname in the UK, so why would Victor Collier now call himself Marek Bartosz" Shivi said.

"It's something we did talk about much earlier if you remember, a person can change his name by deed poll, they may not be married, I don't know, but it doesn't matter, I am convinced that it is Collier" Dan said.

"How sure are you about his signet ring and the initials VC" Billy said, *"did you get a real close up when you shook hands".*

"I'm pretty sure Billy, but I am going to see Collier's mother again and see what she says, I need it confirmed independently. I did promise if we got any information about Victor, we would let her know.

Sam said, "Assuming you get that confirmed by Mrs Collier, where do we go from there as far as approaching them both to get to the bottom of what if anything they did know, and why they both left Manchester shortly after the murder".

"Let's see what Mrs Collier has to say first eh, then I will see how the boss wants to play it", Billy said. *"Ideally, I suppose if we can get them back here to interview them it would be better still. Dan, you go ahead and see what Victor's mother says".*

Shivi said, *"Can I ask a question Dan, why do you still call your old army boss Captain, and not by his name now both of you are finished with the military, do you actually know his name".*

Dan laughed and explained, *"Force of habit Shivi, yes, I do know his full name, but in our unit, we were encouraged to get into the habit of* **not** *using names for security reasons. You may have seen an old TV programme called Dad's Army; it was a comedy featuring the Home Guard and one classic line included a German senior officer demanding to know one of the young Home Guards names, and the young chap's own Captain shouted* **Don't tell him Pike**, *well it was sort of like that.*

Sam and Billy both laughed out loud and said, *"Yes, I remember that".*

"Shivi, get the updated info on these other witnesses who worked at the Council and were interviewed and gave statements at the time. We need to speak to them again. Sam, you liaise with Shivi and see if you can set up some interviews" Billy said.

As Dan pulled up outside Rose Colliers house, he could see her tending the tiny patch of garden area at the front. She presented a tired lonely looking lady who had aged before her time.

She was surprised to see Dan again and invited him inside with a half worried look on her face.

"Thanks for seeing me Mrs Collier, if you remember when we last met, I promised I would let you know if we had any information about Victor" Dan began, *"I just wanted to ask a few more questions".*

He knew he had to hear about the ring from her independently without him first mentioning it, so he started by saying, *"How tall would you say Victor is?".*

"Oh, I would say around five foot six or seven, he never was very tall even into adulthood, why do you ask", she replied looking a little perplexed.

"Blue eyes, like yours Mrs Collier" Dan continued as if being complimentary, *"Any distinguishing features?"*

"Like what" she answered, now looking really concerned.

"I just mean tattoos and the like that would be visible, or does he always wear any jewellery, a neck chain or the like". Dan continued.

At this, Rose Collier slumped back in her chair and said, *"No please God, don't tell me he is dead, you have found a body haven't you".*

Dan realised how this must have sounded and was immediately sorry he had chosen those words and said, *"No, no Mrs Collier, I believe we have located Victor who is very much alive and well but wanted to be sure we have the right person. I have seen him and spoken to him, he looks very well indeed rest assured".*

Once she had regained some composure Dan continued, *"I had not intended to upset you, I am sorry, but we have to ask those kinds of questions to confirm identity".*

"Well Mr Nichols, I can confirm that my son has indeed got my eyes and he has no distinguishing marks or features, and he has never been a medallion man", then as if as an afterthought she said,*" When he was eighteen, I bought him a gold signet ring and had his initial engraved on it, he wears it on his right hand next to his little finger, is that enough detail for you Mr Nichols".*

That was all Dan wanted to hear and said with an inward sigh of relief, *"Now I can tell you we have his address, and not only does he look very well Mrs Collier, but I believe you may be a grandmother".*

All this was too much for the poor lady who then broke down in tears.

After recovering from the shock of what Dan had told her, a sort of surreal but welcome sense of calm seemed to drift into the room, after which a lengthy conversation followed when over a cup of tea Dan was able to explain why they had located Victor, and more importantly why they felt it was important to speak to him regarding his time with Mr Dorsey and why he had gone to the trouble of changing his name.

Mrs Collier could offer no explanation as to why Victor had acted so strangely and decided to leave after Dorsey's murder, but it was clear she was desperate to know why herself. She also confirmed that her son does have an occasional stutter particularly when he felt stressed, she had put this down to his father's bullying when Victor was a child.

He thanked Mrs Collier for her help and as he got up to leave, she said. *"Will I be able to see him Mr Nichols"?*

"I am going to do my best to make that happen" Dan replied as he shook her hand and said goodbye, leaving Mrs Collier reading the only letter she had received from her son Victor in all these years.

Dan immediately rang Billy with the ID confirmation as soon as he got in his car.

"I'll tell the boss when you get back Dan, that is great news, see you tomorrow" Billy said.

CHAPTER 30

Shivi seemed to be shuffling around in his chair constantly shifting his position while sitting in front of his screen, much to the annoyance of Billy who had been scribbling his notes in preparation of going to give DI Morris the Victor Collier news.

After losing concentration and screwing up some of his half-written attempts, Billy threw them across the room at Shivi and said, *"What the hell's up with you this morning Shivi, have you got Nobby Stiles or something".*

"What, who's Nobby Stiles" Shivi said spinning around.

"He means piles Shivi, you know, haemorrhoids", Harry Styles" Sam said.

Shivi jumped up from his chair looking at the threadbare seat covering and said, *"haemorrhoids, what are haemorrhoids, what do they look like?".*

Billy burst out laughing saying, *"He thinks they are bugs, thank goodness he didn't choose a career in the medical profession eh".*

Sam being more practically minded than her three male companions had brought a cushion in from home after her very first day in the office. Her cushion cover design looked like there were lots of little letter S's on it and she liked to think they looked like her own name initial for Sam. To say that all their chairs were second hand would be an understatement.

"Shivi, look take my cushion, I've got another one at home, I'm off to see if I can speak to a couple of the Council staff who gave statements at the time. Look the covers got you initial S for Shivi on it".

Now with some quiet returning to the office Dan explained to Billy in detail how he had managed to get into the London address with the great help of Captain and his man Tim Symonds and why he was convinced they had found the correct Krystna Bartosz and Victor Collier. Billy had listened in complete silence right to the end then said, *"That was quite a plan Dan, Dan with a plan eh, I will go and fill the boss in now, well done".*

With now just Dan and Shivi in the office Dan started to wonder how they could approach Collier and Bartosz again to explain the real reason they wanted to speak to them, and why it had been necessary to use subterfuge to locate and identify them.

Dan's thoughts were interrupted when Shivi started chuckling to himself, then gave out a laugh.

"What's so funny", Dan said.

"I've just looked it up, haemorrhoids, piles, that's funny, Harry Styles eh, that is funny".

Dan just raised his eyebrows, shook his head, and got on with his thoughts.

After about half an hour the door swung open, and Billy noisily backed into the office clearly carrying something. Dan jumped up and held the door open for him. When he swung around, he was holding an office chair.

"Here you are Shivi, a present for you from DI Morris", Billy said when he got his breath back.

The chair looked brand new, and Shivi couldn't believe it.

"Come on then, how's that for size, how did you wangle that Billy", Dan said as Shivi plonked himself down and swung around like a kid with a new toy.

"Ways and means act dear boy, ways and means act", Billy replied in his best Noel Coward voice impression. *"Actually, when I told the boss about his haemorrhoids, he said there were a couple of spare office chairs in the typing pool, and we could take one".*

After things had settled down Dan asked Billy what the boss had said about the Victor Collier news, and how he thought we could best approach it from here.

"He said even if you are right, we can't arrest him for changing his name or having a bit of a stutter, neither of them have committed any offence as far as we know, so he suggested we go and formally interview them and take their statements".

"So, in other words, sort it out yourself", Dan said.

"Well not quite Billy replied, *"he suggested that Sam should liaise with the local Station in their area, and that she attends with a local officer to do the interviews, the boss said he will set that up. I think that is actually a very good idea Dan, I'm sure that Sam will be up for it and there will be no reason for Collier and Bartosz to connect Sam's visit with your earlier one".*

"I would never have thought of that Billy, it's a great idea, I guess that's why Mike is a DI then eh" Dan said.

When Sam arrived back to the office with the follow up of her contacting a couple of the original witnesses, she reminded Dan that that one of the former Council staff who had given a statement at the time is called Charlotte Clayton. Sam had managed to speak to this lady who had worked directly under Councillor Holroyd in the Finance Department as his sort of number two, his secretary.

She told Sam that she had left the job around two months after Dorsey's murder. A spinster now aged 60, Charlotte Clayton came across to Sam as quite strait-laced and very much old school.

Sam had asked if there was any particular reason why she left the job, and her answer surprised Sam. She stated that there were certain matters she felt uneasy about. When asked to explain more, she rather reluctantly said that some payment transactions which passed her desk were for invoices which appeared to be duplicated or unaccounted for, and Holroyd had authorised payment of them despite this.

When she had raised this with Holroyd, he had just dismissed it as not important and nothing for her to worry about. Sam asked why she hadn't mentioned this in her original statement.

Charlotte said when interviewed by the Police at the time, their questions were all about Mr Dorsey, and how well she knew him and if she had ever been to his studio, they appeared to be stock questions, and she was never asked any questions at all about Councillor Holroyd.

Some of her other co-workers who had given statements had said they were also asked the exact same questions.

It was only later when she thought about her visit by the Police she became nervous, as one of the invoices that appeared to be duplicated quite a few times was from Mr Dorsey, and she had not mentioned any of this, she then began to worry that if the Police were to inspect the accounts and this come to light, she wanted to disassociate herself with anything untoward or worse even appear to be implicated with any wrong doing, and that is why she decided to leave the Council job.

That wasn't all Sam explained, when she asked Charlotte Clayton if these payments were just to Mr Dorsey she said, no there was one other name that some unaccounted payments were made to, someone called Zac Gold.

Billy froze, then said, "Zac Gold, are you sure this other person was called Zac Gold Sam?".

"Absolutely certain Billy, she has signed to verify that today, look", Sam replied producing the latest statement.

"Something odd was clearly going on back prior to Dorsey's murder, Holroyd's son Jonathan discovers all this strange activity that was going on when looking through his late father's communications between the Councillor himself, Dorsey ***and*** *this fella called Zac Gold. What a pity we had to pass that laptop and all that paper record file upstairs eh, who the hell is this mysterious Zac Gold"* Dan said.

Billy was now panicking a bit and wondering if he should take this additional news referring to Gold to DI Morris, and playing for thinking time he said, *"Yes, it is a pity we didn't get chance to have a look at that stuff on the laptop"*.

During all this time Shivi had stayed quiet, then with a sheepish look on his face said, *"Actually before you took the stuff to DI Morris, I did a quick copy of the paperwork and extracted some stuff off the laptop on a memory stick, but I haven't looked at it as you told us to leave this part of the investigation to the top dogs up above"*.

"What do you reckon we should do Billy" Dan said.

"Leave it with me" Billy replied still thinking on his feet, *"let's see if we can get Bartosz and hopefully Victor Collier interviewed in London first"*, then he explained to Sam that DI Morris was arranging for her to pay the London address a visit with a PC from the local station down there.

"All in all, it's been a fairly active day eh Billy", Dan said as the two made their way out of the station.

After an unusual silence Dan finally said, *"Something on your mind".*

"Fancy a quick beer at the Crown and Anchor Dan, there's something I wanted to mention", Billy said.

Now sat in the corner of their old HQ, which had always provided an inspirational thinking hub where the two old pals had spent so much time going over the evidence they had successfully uncovered as civilians before being seconded to DI Mike Morris's Police Cold Case Review team Dan said, *"Well come on the suspense is killing me, what is it that's bothering you".*

"I'll go and get the drinks in first Dan", Billy said and wandered over to the bar.

When he got back Billy said, *"That new barman is beginning get on my nerves".*

"Is that it then, that's what you wanted to mention to me, that's what's been on your mind, the new barman's getting on your nerves" Dan said.

"He's Welsh" Billy replied.

"Oh, well that explains everything, the barman is Welsh" Dan said.

"No, he keeps calling me Boyo, and he repeats everything".

"What are you going on about" Dan said, *"You are getting on my nerves now.*

"Well, when I just ordered two beers, he said in his annoying Welsh accent, so two beers is it boyo? then when he got them he said here you are boyo, two beers isn't it. Billy replied.

"Well now you've got that off your chest, what is really bothering you" Dan said.

After a few swigs of his beer Billy said, *"You know when we got the information and laptop from Jonathan Holroyd that he found after his dad died, and I took everything up to the boss and said I had told him that we had enough on our hands and persuaded him to let the IT experts to deal with it, well I was being economical with the truth Dan".*

After listening in silence to what had really happened and what DI Morris and DCI Gill had told Billy, Dan said, *"A bent Scotland Yard accountant, and there's still millions missing, well I can understand why they want to keep that quiet, does this Zac Gold fella exist do they know".*

"Well, what they do know is that the missing millions are still out there somewhere Dan".

"Best get Shivi to delete that laptop stuff on his memory sticks then eh Billy?".

Neither said a word but looked at each other and were clearly thinking the same thing.

Dan picked up the two empty glasses to head to the bar and whispered in Billy's ear, *"Maybe just a peek at that laptop stuff eh, two beers is it then boyo".*

CHAPTER 31

The information Shivi had extracted from the memory stick and the content in some of the hidden files provided even more insight of what was beginning to look like an illegal money investment scam involving the bent Scotland Yard accountant, known only as Peter, Councillor Holroyd, Dorsey and the mysterious Zac Gold.

The later exchanges appeared to be complaints by Holroyd and Dorsey to the accountant Peter, that their investments had not produced his iron clad promised high returns, in fact there had been no return at all, and they were becoming impatient.

Peter had then sent some reassuring emails saying that Zac Gold had promised their payments within a week.

If it was a sort of pyramid scam, Holroyd and Dorsey could well have encouraged other investors who could now be breathing down their necks and the emails were becoming more threatening.

Looking at the dates, it looked like by this time, the Scotland Yard accountant Peter had been bubbled and arrested and communications from him had stopped.

Dorsey was then sending emails direct to Zac Gold with ultimatums, stating that unless his initial investment of several million, plus the assured substantial dividend was not paid into his bank account within one week, the whole scam would be exposed and furthermore Dorsey stated he had connections with the Manchester underworld, and he would make sure Zac Gold would pay.

This was heavy stuff and a lot to take in. Billy stressed that all this should not go beyond the four walls of their office, not even to DI Morris at this stage.

In the meantime, arrangements had been made for DC Sam Brown to travel to London and link up with a local plod and interview Krystna Bartosz.

There were just two more of the original Town Hall witnesses to see and Dan was to deal with those, but Shivi had found that one of them had since passed away, but Dan said he would see if the widow may be worth speaking to anyway. However, he just couldn't stop thinking about this latest discovery of emails and the likely investment scam. Who was behind it, who was the architect?

It transpired that the first witness Dan spoke to had only worked in the Council offices for a short time and genuinely had not known Dorsey and only knew as most did, that Dorsey's Photography Studio covered all the official civic formal occasions for the Town Hall's records etc.

When Dan arrived at the other original witness's address, hoping to speak to the widow he got no reply. Just as he was about to leave, a small car pulled up and a smartly dressed lady got out and asked if she could help. Her appearance reflected the tidy appearance of the semi-detached house frontage situated in a neat little cul de sac.

Dan produced his ID and explained the purpose of his call to which the lady readily identified herself as Margaret Farrel the widow of John Farrel who had been employed at the Town Hall and she invited him into the house.

Dan explained that all the previous witness statements were being checked by the Cold Case Review team for detail and accuracy, and said he hoped that speaking to her about her late husband was not too much of an imposition or upsetting for her. Her reaction, or lack of it seemed a bit odd.

Margaret Farrel was quite thin and tall, with swept back fair hair greying slightly, and very well spoken, and it came as no surprise to Dan that the interior of the house was equally as neat and tidy as the outside. A proud woman he guessed.

Rather than read out her late husband's very short statement, Dan thought he would let Mrs Farrel read it herself and thus try to observe her reactions and comments if any.

She read it in silence then looked up at Dan, and then read it through again before handing it back to Dan without saying a word.

"Well, would you say from your knowledge that your husband's statement is accurate Mrs Farrel?" Dan said.

She took the statement from him again and looking at it said to

Dan's complete surprise, *"No it is not accurate Mr Nichols, in fact it is a complete fabrication, when he says in his statement of* ***truth,*** (and she emphasized the word truth) *it is an out and out lie, he was good at lies Mr Nichols".*

Up until this point Mrs Farrel had remained calm and courteous but clearly Dan's direct question touched a nerve, and her calmness turned to anger, obviously all had not been sunshine and roses between Mrs and Mrs Farrel.

"Would you like to elaborate on that Mrs Farrel"? Dan asked.

"Well despite him stating that he didn't really know Dorsey very well and had never been to his studio, he was a member of Dorsey's so called evening Aphrodite Club, along with the other supposed pillars of the local community. He actually paid to ogle at naked young women and take photographs of them whilst drinking sometimes to excess", she replied, now getting into full flow after getting all this off her chest.

"And that supposed ever so respectable Mr snooty Councillor Holroyd was just as bad as Dorsey", She spat out. *"I never knew if my husband had cheated on me physically, but he certainly did mentally"* she continued.

After a short silence she said tearfully, *"I am sorry Mr Nichols, I didn't mean to lose my temper like that".*

Dan said, *"Please Mrs Farrel, I know this must have been very difficult for you, but thank you for being so frank and honest, I will leave you in peace now".*

Dan certainly hadn't expected that when he set off from the office, and this new revelation was another piece of the jigsaw which put together Peter the bent accountant, his assumed business partner Zac Gold, Councillor Holroyd and the murdered photographer Arnold Frederick Dorsey. What were they up to and who was influencing who in this investment scam.

On the drive back Dan started to focus on that thought and tried to figure out how it all could have started.

As they now knew, money embezzled from the Scotland Yard's seized drug money by their own accountant, was used by him to buy himself a luxury property, but that property was seized, and the money was recovered under the Process of Crimes Act. However, that still left several million still unaccounted for with the now dead accountant claiming he invested it with a man called Zac Gold, an American stockbroker.

Did this Zac Gold exist or was Peter the accountant simply transferring the embezzled money into an overseas account in this false name in order that he would still have access to it when he had served his five-year prison sentence. The fact that he died in prison after 18 months means the missing millions are still out there in a secret unknown overseas account.

Dan's mind was working overtime, this was complex to say the least.

By the time he had arrived back at the office he had decided in his mind to press the rewind button, go back to the start and try to look further into the Scotland Yard accountant and his supposed relationship with the mysterious Zac Gold.

CHAPTER 32

It was pleasantly quiet in the office when Dan arrived the next morning, Sam was on her way to London and Billy had rung in to say he had someone to see.

Dan pulled out all the information they had so far on the reported relationship between the four people seemingly involved in the investment scam, three of whom were dead, and one possibly fictitious.

After going over everything again he said to Shivi, *"Can you see if you can get any information at all on these seminars held specifically and solely for financial heads of Government Departments. We know they took place in London every six months and were designed apparently to work on how to utilise the best of Government funding and share proven successful policies. Maybe these types of seminars don't exist anymore, but we know they did prior to our murder".*

"10-4 Dan will do" Shivi replied.

Wonder what Billy is up to he thought as he again went over the information in silence, just in case he had missed something.

The silence was short lived as Billy came in with a big grin on his face.

"You won the lottery or something", Dan said.

"Not quite Danny boy, I heard rumour that the Turd had been arrested and was just checking it out, seems there will be a piece in tonight's paper. Headline Eddie is taking the credit for his undercover reporters passing details on to the Police about some local thieving and drug dealing".

"Good old Eddie then eh? Dan said. Then after a while he said, "I keep meaning to ask you Billy, when you got that new chair for Shivi from upstairs the other day, did you happen to see Paula".

"I did as it happens, and had quite a chat, she asked about you if that's what you are getting at", Billy said.

"No, I was just thinking it might be nice if we all met up again at the Bull one night, we quite enjoyed it didn't we".

"Well, you certainly did, that was obvious" Billy replied with a grin on his face.*" Why don't you ask her, she will probably be on her lunch break now"*

he said looking at his watch.

To Billy's complete surprise Dan said, *"Do you know, I think I will"* and without further ado got up and left. Even Shivi spun round from his screen in surprise.

While he was away, Shivi got on with trying to research these financial seminars held in London.

Dan arrived back and said, *"Apparently a note has been left at the front desk for PC Oliver, you better go and see Billy".*

The desk Sergeant on duty was Jack Barker. It seemed like Jack had worked at the station for ever, almost part of the furniture. He was known for greeting every caller with a broad smile but could quickly change if he got an awkward customer and was once almost sacked

for throwing an argumentative mouthy fella out the front door for complaining about justice, or the lack of it, but not before allegedly saying how's this for justice and kicking the fella up the arse.

"Eh up Jack, I thought you had retired" Billy said.

"Can't get anyone to take my place Billy, you don't fancy the job do you", he replied as he handed over a grubby folded bit of paper.

Billy looked at the note and frowned, *"When did this come in Jack".*

"Don't know to be honest, I only came on this morning, obviously can't be important, it wasn't logged when I looked first thing and only spotted the note on the shelf below a few minutes ago".

Billy remained puzzled as he looked at the note again and said, *"Cheers Jack, keep taking those ugly pills eh".*

Back in the office, *"What was all that about then Billy, one of your admiring fans from the open mike nights at the Golden Ball".*

Billy still looking puzzled said, *"I'm just popping out Dan, will explain later.*

On his way to the railway arches Billy looked at the note again, it was from Polish Joe and simply read, urgent, need to see you.

When he got there, there was no sign of old Angus or his tatty old armchair.

Joe appeared almost immediately. *"Where's Angus Joe, is he alright?"*

"He's gone" Joe replied, *"Three days ago, struggled to breath and passed away in the night, I stayed with him but couldn't help and finally got a passer-by to call an ambulance, when it arrived, they said he was already dead".* Joe said struggling a bit.

Billy for once was stuck for words. *"Three days ago? I only got your note today, I am so sorry, is there anything I can do Joe, anything".*

"I know he would have wanted you to have this" Joe replied and handed Billy the small accordion concertina.

"What about a funeral has anyone said what would happen".

"A man came and said he was from some local office and said there will just be a small cremation as there were no known relatives" Joe replied.

"Thanks Joe, I guess you will miss him eh", Billy said as he shook hands and left.

On his way back to the station Billy called in at the Public Administration Office where a member of staff confirmed what Polish Joe had told him and said there will be a simple ceremony and crematorium as soon as possible which would be paid for at public expense.

That night in the Crown and Anchor Billy told Dan about old Angus and they raised a glass to him.

This was also the first chance Dan had to explain all about his interview with the widow Margaret Farrel and how John Farrel's original statement was anything but the truth. *"Oh what a tangled web we weave when first we practice to deceive eh",* Dan said.

"Another of your famous quotes eh" Billy said sarcastically as he got up to go to the bar.

When he came back with the beers he said, *"Eh, did you notice that bloody annoying Welsh fella wasn't serving behind the bar Dan".*

"Yeh, never thought anything of it, why".

"Well, he's only been sacked", Billy said with a broad grin, *"Apparently some of the locals couldn't understand a word he said, then he started*

mumbling in Welsh, they thought he was swearing at them, and one took a swing at him, shame we missed all that eh?".

"Anyway, now you are in a more cheerful mood, what do you think about the goings on with the investment scam Billy, Dorsey was up to his neck in it as well as Holroyd, Peter the Met accountant and Zac Gold if he exists. I think we need to go back to how these four characters came to get entangled with each other".

"Good idea Sherlock" Billy said.

"Leave it with me Watson, I've already got Shivi trying to see if he can dig up any research on these seminars in London, so we'll see what he comes up with.

"Remember, we can't tell the boss yet, so I guess we will have to keep plugging away and try to figure out what did happen Danny boy, oh, and by the way you never told me if you did speak to Paula earlier".

"I did indeed and have arranged to meet up with her on Friday night for a drink, I've got her phone number now" Dan said looking pleased with himself.

"You little devil, anywhere nice, the Grand Hotel or that new posh restaurant that's opened up in the old Stock Exchange building".

"Actually, I was going to speak to you about that Billy, just wondered if you and Jenny might want to make up a foursome", Dan said now not sounding quite as confident.

"As it happens, I am meeting up with Jenny on Friday, but It's only at the Golden Ball, I've got to see Dougie to talk about the reopening of the upstairs room for our next open mike night.

"That's fine Billy. We will meet you there then and the girls can get to know each other". Dan said immediately, sounding almost relieved.

CHAPTER 33

"*Detective Constable Sam Brown, pleased to meet you*" Sam said as she shook hands with the fresh-faced uniformed PC in London who was to accompany her to speak with Krystna Bartosz.

Despite the uncomfortable journey into London, Sam looked as immaculate as ever in a dark blue jacket with matching skirt and sparkling white blouse. Her neat haircut and trim figure clearly a surprise to the young man standing in front of her.

"PC Johnson ma'am", he replied politely touching the rim of his helmet in an old fashion respectful way, a helmet which looked slightly too big for him.

Sam could tell that this young man had clearly been expecting a male DC, but she was well used to that by now. *"No need to call me ma'am, makes me sound like your grandmother, just call me Sam, short for Samantha as I'm sure you already guessed. What do your colleagues call you PC Johnson?".*

"They just call me Ginger ma'am, I mean Sam" he replied.

"OK, I assume you have been briefed as to why I am here, so this is what we are going to do Ginger".

Sam then explained the purpose of the visit to speak to Krystna Bartoz and told him he would be present to demonstrate that this was a formal Police matter and that she would do the talking, and he should simply observe unless she instructed him otherwise.

With Dan's detailed account of his own pretext visit fresh in her mind Sam and "Ginger" arrived at the house where the call was eventually answered by a quite short, slightly overweight dark-haired female aged around thirty and fitting perfectly the description Dan had provided of Krystna Bartosz.

Her reaction wasn't surprising considering the visit was not pre-arranged and the panic on her face was immediate, *"what is wrong, has there been an accident"* she said as she saw the uniformed officer.

"No nothing like that madam" Sam said reassuringly, *"we simply need to*

speak with Krystna Bartoz who formally lived in Manchester some years ago, do we have the right address".

"Yes, I am Krystna Bartoz, and yes I did move from Manchester some time ago, what is this about and how can I help". She replied looking around nervously to check if any neighbours were watching before inviting them inside.

Once inside and seated, PC Johnson took off his helmet which revealed exactly why he was known as Ginger as he exposed the neatest short bright red haircut Sam had ever seen. She tried to disguise her surprise with a little cough to clear her throat before she spoke.

"Just to be certain Krystna, did you know a businessman called Mr. Dorsey who had a photographic studio in Manchester going back some ten years ago". Sam asked as she took out her pocket notebook.

"Yes, I did, and I worked part time for a while as a cleaner for him at his studio" she replied.

I'm sure we didn't know that Sam thought to herself.

"I think you will know that Mr Dorsey was found murdered in his studio, and to this day the person who committed this crime has never been found. I don't know if you are aware, but the case is being reinvestigated by a cold case review team in Manchester and those who knew Mr Dorsey are being spoken to again".

Krystna Bartosz was now looking very uncomfortable and nervously playing with her hands and kept looking at her watch.

"If this is a bad time, we can arrange for you to come into the station as there is a lot of details to go through Krystna" Sam said.

"Well, that would be best really, my daughter is at college and may be home anytime", She replied.

"OK, we can arrange that but just a quick couple of questions first and then we will leave you for today. If I can just take your full name and date of birth and your contact telephone number, please".

After taking down the details Sam said, *"And place of birth?".*

"I was born in Poland, a suburb of Warsaw. I came to the UK with my mother when I was a baby, will that be all now?".

"Just one more thing Krystna, I see you gave a statement at the time which confirmed that a Victor Collier was with you at the time of the murder. We know that Mr Collier also worked for Mr Dorsey. We have spoken to his mother Rose Collier quite recently and she told us that you and Victor were friends and that shortly after the murder Victor left home and moved South.

We still need to speak to Victor, but his mother never had an address for him, she explained that sadly he only wrote to her once since leaving, and there was no return address. She was quite distraught and didn't even know if her only son was dead or alive. Just imagine, that must be awful don't you think, so if by chance you do hear from Victor can you ask him to contact me, I would love to tell Mrs Collier he is OK. As a mother yourself I'm sure you will know what I mean.

We will of course need to speak to you again in much more detail in the next few days", and with that Sam gave Krystna Bartosz her card.

On the way back to the station Sam thanked PC Ginger Johnson and asked him what he thought about the interview.

"She was obviously very nervous, particularly when you started to talk about Victor Collier, and she was clearly anxious to get rid of us.

I wonder who the men's size 8 brown shoes belong to that were on the floor just to the right of the lounge door".

"That was very observant of you Ginger, how do you know they are size 8", Sam said.

"Because I am size 9 and I purposely put my right foot alongside them on the way out. Maybe she was concerned that the gentleman owner of those shoes was due to come home, not her daughter".

You don't' know how close to the truth you were, Sam thought to herself.

"I am impressed PC Ginger Johnson; you are going to make a good detective one day I am sure".

During the train journey back to Manchester Sam was hoping that her formal Police approach would prove sufficient to prompt a positive reaction from Krystna Bartosz and that she would not simply try to go to ground along with Collier as they clearly had tried to do shortly after Dorsey's murder. There had to be a reason for that, and they had to find out what that reason was.

Her woman's instinct was telling her that once Victor knew about today's interview, she could hear from them both and hopefully soon.

It wasn't long before Sam's instinct turned out to be right, as even before the train had reached Wigan Krystna rang her.

She said that after Sam had left, she had searched through some old paperwork and found a mobile number for Victor Collier and had managed to speak to him. She said she had told Victor about today's Police visit and he said he would be happy to speak to the Police.

That was not all, Victor had said was going to travel to see his mother, and Krystna said they would travel to Manchester together as they both would like to speak to the Case Review Team direct.

Just wait until I tell them back at the office Sam thought as she sat back in her seat smiling to herself as she stared out of the carriage window and feeling just a little bit smug.

CHAPTER 34

Dan sat back in his favourite chair at home with a glass of whisky on hand preparing to look through the folder Shivi had prepared for him about the mirky investment scam involving Dorsey and co.

During his military career as an intelligence officer Dan had found that occasional solitude and even isolation sometimes provided him with a space in which he could concentrate on an issue without the distraction of other things going on around him. He was determined to use this time to analyse what they already knew, and what other information Shivi's research had come up with.

He was quite surprised just how Shivi had managed to delve back to even the slightest information about the London seminars which were designed strictly for senior finance personnel working for Government departments going back to the period prior to Dorsey's murder.

Somehow, he had sourced back dated programmes and literature which described the seminar topics and the listed expert speakers.

There was no list of the actual attendees, but it was already known that Peter the bent Met accountant and Councillor Holroyd had certainly attended and met here.

The email evidence from Holroyd's laptop shows that Dorsey had been recruited into the investment scheme and the fact that there was discord, and even threatening messages certainly justified the cold case team's continued efforts to see if there was any further evidence that could point to Dorsey's murderer, despite their direct order from above **not** to investigate this aspect any further.

Just like an infection that spreads, the only way to resolve this was to get to the actual source of the issue and discover where and how the infection/scam started.

There were certainly very well qualified speakers looking through the list including even former Bank of England advisers and professors of economics.

To simplify matters Dan decided to make a list of all the speakers names along with their speciality topics and the titles of their subject presentations.

He then went through the information again and made a note alongside each name with the number of times those experts had appeared. Most seemed to have appeared only once with just a few who had been asked to speak more than once.

One name stood out as clearly being popular, as Professor J. Clifford had spoken at the seminar several times. Dan made a note of the dates and the titles of his presentations. With no list of attendees Dan thought it seemed a reasonable place to start.

He did a quick laptop search on Professor J Clifford which confirmed he was a lecturer of economics at Oxford University. He had also published a book on business economics entitled *"Change"* and had written a thesis which had appeared in some industry publications.

Time for a whisky top up before delving a little further. Looking over the dates that the professor had been the speaker he noticed that it was a regular slot, in fact every four months, up until after a certain date when it stopped, and his name never appeared again. Maybe he retired or even passed away. Still, he thought at least there was a reasonable chance that Councillor Holroyd and the Scotland Yard accountant would have attended some of these presentations together and where they would likely to have met.

Maybe Shivi would be able to have another go at trying to get more information but in the meantime, Dan found one of the industry publications online which did include Professor Clifford's thesis, but Dan's eyes were beginning to go by then. The thesis was also entitled *"Change"*. He was just too tired to start reading the piece so that would have to wait until tomorrow.

Just before he called it a night, he noticed a couple of reviews on the thesis in the same magazine written by some of the professor's industry contemporaries which seemed quite critical, one suggested his thesis was totally unworkable by suggesting some business procedures and timings would benefit from switching the approach, i.e. reversing accepted work protocols and questioning why should it always be done that way, in effect suggesting there could be advantages doing some things sometimes "the opposite way around" from what had traditionally always been done. One even described the professor's ideas as weird.

Lights out then and more reading tomorrow.

He was looking forward to seeing Paula tomorrow night, they were meeting up with Billy and Jenny at the Golden Ball before going on for a meal. Billy had said he would book a nice table at an Italian restaurant where he said he knew the owner.

Despite the tiredness and the pleasant thought of getting to know Paula more, all this latest investment scam stuff was still swirling around in his mind before Dan finally drifted off.

CHAPTER 35

He hadn't made any written notes the night before, but some of what Dan had remembered still niggled him, and he was going to refresh all his thinking today. He remembered the name of the book Professor Clifford had written, *Change,* and decided to call into the Central Library on his way into the station to see if they had a copy.

When he arrived at the office Sam had just started recounting the details of her successful trip to London, and since she had arrived back had even heard again from Krystna Bartosz informing her that she and Victor Collier were going to travel to Manchester at the weekend and wanted to call in to see them at the station on Monday.

"Great result Sam", Billy said, *"Looks like you pressed all the right buttons, and they clearly have something to tell us, eh? Let's go up and give the boss something to smile about".*

"Yep, you handled that really well Sam" Dan added.

While they were gone, Dan pulled out the library copy of Professor Clifford's book and asked Shivi if he thought there was the likelihood of any other sources he could research about the seminars, in particular any reference to any of the actual attendees. If the investment scam did start here how many others could be victims.

"I'm not hopeful Dan, but I will give it a go" Shivi replied.

Dan took the opportunity of the quiet office time to have a look through the library book he had managed to pick up on the way in.

Strange title, *Change*. Most people have a good look at the front and back covers of books before they buy or get from a library and Dan was no different, that is other than the fact that he also always looked for the page which was normally headed "About the Author" Interesting reading he thought, the professors father had fled to the UK as a Jewish immigrant from Germany to escape the war and obviously had a great influence over his son.

After a short while Shivi said, *"Hey, what do you think about this Dan, I've had another look at the stuff I copied from Councillor Holroyd's laptop onto the memory stick and found another folder tucked away, this may help.*

There is what appears to be a small chat group with exchanges from Holroyd, the Met accountant Peter and two other people who all refer to one of the seminar speakers. They are talking about the last seminar they attended in which a Professor Clifford was the speaker. They all thought his suggestions had become a bit strange with some of his latest reverse ideas.

His views even appeared to be quite critical of some of the financial leaders' economic qualifications and capabilities and questioned whether some should be in such an important position of controlling public funds.

What's more the little group had seemingly all messaged the professor direct to express their opposing views".

"I had forgotten about the laptop Shivi, that's great, can you do a printout of the exchanges please", Dan said.

This is interesting Dan thought and ties in with the adverse reviews about the professor's thesis.

Just then Billy and Sam arrived back from telling the boss about Bartosz and Collier.

"You had better make yourself scarce when they do come in on Monday Dan, they will recognise you and we don't want to spook them, they obviously have got something to tell us", Billy said.

Sam had got DI Morris's OK to go and see Rose Collier again and explain that they now had confirmation that her son Victor was alive and well and living in the London area.

It was one of those calls that instead of turning up on someone's doorstep with bad news, it felt good to be the bearer of good news, and Rose Collier's reaction, despite bursting into tears, was one that Sam would remember.

Whilst she had a strong feeling that Rose would get a visit from Victor, having not seen nor heard from him in all these years, Sam resisted the temptation of suggesting this.

It had been a quite productive week for the team, and all were looking forward to a weekend off.

"Don't forget, seven o'clock sharp at the Golden Ball Danny boy, and do me a favour, don't put that cheap aftershave on, it turned my beer flat last time and it definitely won't impress Paula", Billy said as they left the office.

On his way home Dan realised he hadn't seen Alice from the ground floor apartment for a while and decided to just give her a knock on the way in.

At aged 86, Alice always looked smart, and she seemed genuinely pleased see Dan and invited him inside. Her place was still neat and tidy as he expected with photos of her late husband and the horses, they used to have years ago proudly displayed on a shiny clean old, wooded sideboard.

"Just thought I would say a quick hello Alice, how are you?".

"I'm OK Dan, just short of company theses day, the joys of getting old I suppose eh, would you like a cup of tea?".

"I can't' tonight Alice but will try to pop and see you a bit more often I promise, I will soon have more time on my hands. I guess it feels lonely now with both apartments on the ground floor still being empty since Owen died and Kevin went to prison".

"I still can't believe Kevin could have been so unkind to me Dan, I thought he was my friend, when all the time he was a partner in the awful horse charity scam. Yes, it does seem a bit lonely at times but Tammy occasionally pop in when her hospital shifts allow, that poor girl does work so hard, and Jean helps me with my weekly shopping so I can't complain".

"I see Kevin's old flat is still showing the To Let sign, has there been any interest at all do you know?" Dan asked.

"Not as far as I know but I suppose the flat is like mine, ideal for single occupancy so will only appeal to a person who lives alone. Still, it would be nice to have a neighbour next door".

"Just a thought Alice, do you still go to the day centre, if so, why not mention there's a place going next door to you to Ms Riley, maybe she knows someone?"

"I might just do that Dan, yes, things have settled down after the charity

scam, you remember my friend Doris, who was also taken in by Kevin and his fake charity scheme, well I meet with her once a week, so that it nice".

Dan looked at his watch and said, *"Well must go Alice, I've got a date".*

Alice gave an affectionate smile and said, *"Well you go and enjoy your date Dan".*

After he had showered and started trying to remember where he had put that new aftershave he had bought, never knowing whether Billy had just been winding him up as usual, he suddenly realised what he had said to Alice, *"I've got a date".* He smiled to himself, and it made him feel good.

Dan was really looking forward to seeing Paula, he knew he liked her, but didn't quite know what the attraction was, and was hoping tonight he would get to know her more. He was basically still a quite shy private man, and deep down was glad that Billy and Jenny would be with them tonight.

CHAPTER 36

He had already checked that Paula was fine eating Italian and when he met up with her, she looked really nice, but in a sort of smart classy way and she welcomed Dan with a huge smile.

On their way to the Golden Ball, Dan was trying to think of what to chat about when Paula suddenly linked his arm. It immediately felt so comfortable, and he automatically linked her, and they walked along arm in arm.

Paula made him laugh when she told him about Eve and said as usual just about everyone in their office knew exactly what Eve's busy social life would be over the weekend in every detail. Dan was just about to say, did you know Eve had a brother called Peter Knight, but then thought better of it.

There was no sign of Billy in the lounge at the Golden Ball when they arrived, but Jenny was sat alone at a table near to the bar nursing a half glass of red wine.

"He's upstairs with Dougie checking out the function room hoping it will soon be ready for the monthly open mike Friday nights to start again" Jenny said as they sat down with her. *"You know what he's like when he's in open mike night mode Dan".*

"Jenny, meet Paula, Paula this is Jenny, let me get you girls a drink, looks like he abandoned you a while back Jenny looking at your glass". Dan said.

When he got back to the table, Jenny and Paula were having a good old giggle and clearly getting on like a house on fire.

"We've just been walking down memory lane Dan, our families are from the same general area would you believe", Jenny said.

The atmosphere became even more relaxing as Dan tried to recall some of his and Billy's old schooldays, *"Even Dougie goes back that far with us"*, Dan said as he spotted Dougie and Billy arriving back at the bar area.

"Everything in working order then Billy?" as he sat down to join them Jenny asked.

"Just checking my workstation and the lighting is OK", Billy replied looking quite serious for a change.

"Workstation" Dan muttered to himself under his breath, trying to hide a chuckle.

"He does take all this very seriously you know Paula, but he is very good, will you be coming to the next open mike night then?" Jenny asked.

"Of course she will be here won't you Paula" Billy said, *I'll reserve a special table for you".*

The conversation flowed with all four relaxed and enjoying their Friday night out.

"Where's this Italian restaurant then", Dan said.

It's within strolling distance, it used to be called Garibaldi's, you know after that famous Italian fella Dan".

"I know who Garibaldi was, so what's the place called now then Billy?".

"Baldy Gary's, I have known the owner Gary for years, he's a nice fella".

"Baldy Gary's?". Dan and the girls laughed nearly choking on their drinks. *"Are you winding us up Billy? what's Gary's surname?"*

"His name is Gary Smith", Billy said.

"I bet Gary's family have some distant connection with Italy though, I've been to a few different parts of Italy, it can be beautiful". Dan said trying to bring some semblance of normality back into the conversation.

"No Italian connection, all his family are from Ancoats", Billy said finishing his drink, *"Anyway he is a nice fella, as you will see when we get there, come on let's move on".*

Dan started to think maybe the idea of letting Billy organise the night was not such a good idea after all; this was his first date with Paula, and he wanted it to be special, and it could turn out to be a disaster.

The restaurant was busy already with only a few vacant tables.

"Over here", came the distinct broad Manchester accent of the plump smiling chap who came to greet them and walk them to a neat table in a nice corner. *"Nice to see you Billy and your lovely guests".*

"Jenny, Paula, Dan, this is Gary". Billy said.

"Pleased to finally meet you Gary, we have been hearing all about your restaurant" Dan said as he shook Gary's hand.

Well Gary certainly was bald, he couldn't have been any balder, but his neat little black moustache did portray a sort of Italian look Dan had to admit, even if he looked a bit like a character from The God Father movie.

After Billy tried to impress by trying to interpret some of the menu, which was also printed in Italian, without much success, they all enjoyed the lively atmosphere, and the excellent meal that followed, accompanied by a couple of bottles of Italian wine and with no shortage of pleasant conversation.

Billy had looked at his watch a few times when suddenly, the lights in the roomed dimmed to almost blackout accompanied by a loud drum roll and fanfare music then everyone started clapping.

"Probably someone's birthday cake arriving", Dan whispered to Paula.

The lights came on full blast as Gary arrived from the back of the room playing an accordion and bursting into song with a medley of Italian favourites like *That's Amore, Quando Quando, O Solo Mio* and many more, whilst wandering in and out of the tables, his attempt at an Italian accent, just tinged with a bit of Manchester.

Most of the room were clearly used to this performance and they greeted Gary's musical entertainment with appreciative cheers and whistles, no doubt helped along by the steady flow of alcohol consumed. He looked every part Italian, not quite Garibaldi but certainly Baldy Gary.

All in all, it was a thoroughly enjoyable evening with Paula and Dan laughing and chatting all night. Good old Billy after all then.

"He certainly can sing and play that accordion Billy", Dan said as they finished off their tiny free glass of Limoncello sent over courtesy of Gary.

"I just want to go and have a quick word with Gary", Billy said as the restaurant began gradually emptying.

It was a pleasant evening and when Dan had suggested they get a taxi to take Paula home, she said she would be happy to walk the fairly short distance and enjoy the evening air.

Billy and Jenny had decided on a cab, saying their good nights with kisses all around and Jenny whispering in Paula's ear, *"So I look forward to seeing you on the next open mike night, you will enjoy it, it really is lots of fun, and Billy is very good at running the show, but don't let him hear me saying that or it will go to his head".*

Dan was quite pleased at the opportunity of walking Paula home and was hoping they would link arms again. Paula clearly had the same thought and immediately put her arm through his and they strolled along arm in arm chatting away talking and laughing sharing how much they had enjoyed the evening.

As they neared Paula's place, Dan said, *"I wondered if you were free tomorrow, perhaps to go for a walk, the forecast for the weekend is pretty good, there are a few nice walks around the area where I live and a couple of really nice coffee places".*

"Oh, I'm sorry Dan, it's Saturday and I have promised Eve I would go to her meeting at the church hall with her, she is giving a talk on how to keep the local neighbourhood safe. Just one of her many voluntary activities, as I am sure you will be sick of hearing about by now.

I honestly don't know why I let her talk me into these things, but it is difficult saying no, living so close to her.

What about Sunday though if the offer is still on?"

"Sunday would be fine Paula; I will look forward to it" Dan replied.

They both stood for a second without saying anything, just facing each other, Then Paula gave Dan a hug and a quite long kiss on the cheek and said, *"Thank you for tonight, I did enjoy it, and I will look forward to tomorrow".*

On his long walk home Dan reflected on the whole evening and it made him feel good.

CHAPTER 37

By the time they had stopped off for coffee, Dan and Paula had learned so much about each other on their Sunday stroll around the greener area where Dan's place was.

Paula had been born and raised in the Heaton Park area of North Manchester, something she had shared with Jenny in the restaurant on Friday night. Although the two girls never knew each other at the time, they had lived only miles apart and had chatted about their childhood memories of the green areas of the park and nearby golf course.

She told Dan that their leisurely walk in the small surrounding rural area near to Dan's place had brought back many of those growing up memories and didn't realise there was such a pleasant area so close to where he lived.

Paula had first met her husband to be Roy at college and they met again by accident a few years later and started courting when in their early twenties. Roy had joined the Airforce and after his first posting they realised that they wanted to be with each other and they married and she became a military wife, which meant they had experienced life in several countries, latterly being based in the Falkland Islands.

Sadly, Roy had become quite ill only a few years prior to his retirement time and was urgently flown back to the UK and spent almost twelve months in hospital in London before finally passing away.

Paula said she had been lucky to have such a good marriage with plenty of good memories. They were best friends as well as man and wife, they had common interests, they shared the love of music and reading, Paula also loved doing crossword puzzles and she said they could both sit together for hours listening to music and reading etc. without even speaking. Neither had regretted not having children.

Dan explained how and why he ended up back in his birth city of Manchester after retiring from a full military career, and how he was eventually able to track down his schoolboy pal Billy.

Both had joined the army on the same day but soon their postings meant that they had not seen each other for so many years, Billy having come out of the army early and later joining the Manchester Police.

Along the way, they passed the canal area which gave Dan the opportunity to explain what had happened to his former neighbour Owen and how the sad story had ended.

He told Paula that he came back to Manchester to completely retire and how he eventually met up with Billy. How they eventually found Owen's stolen dog in the church grounds and how they also worked together to solve some of the unexpected issues Dan's new apartment neighbours had up until then kept secret behind their locked doors.

They strolled back to Dan's holding hands and Dan noticed that the ground floor To Let sign had been taken down and he thought he must ask Alice again if she had any news.

Back at Dan's they had another cup of coffee. He had the habit of putting his music on just before he put the kettle on and did the same without thinking.

Looking around the room Paula had noticed Dan's selection of books stacked on a small old-fashioned cabinet top. The book "Change" which he was still reading was left on a chair. The cover displayed a photograph of Oxford, which prompted Paula to laugh and say would you believe despite seeing many so places around the world, she had never actually been to Oxford.

CHAPTER 38

"What time are Collier and Bartosz booked in this morning Billy, Dan said as the team settled in on Monday morning.

"Not until eleven, DI Morris, Sam and I are conducting the interviews. They will be seen separately; you stay down here out of the way Dan, I'm going up to go through everything with Mike now".

When Billy had gone Dan said, *"Sam, you grew up in Ancoats didn't you? "We were at an Italian restaurant on Friday night that used to be called Garibaldi's, but it's now called Baldy Gary's and the owner and his family are from Ancoats, just wonder if you knew him, Gary Smith".*

"I know the restaurant Dan, but don't know the owner, but it doesn't surprise me that his family are from Ancoats".

"Why doesn't it surprise you, Sam?"

"You know, Little Italy" she said, *"Going back to the late 1800's and through to the early 1900's there was an influx of Italian immigrants to Manchester, and they made their home in Ancoats, which quickly became known as Little Italy.*

They were very enterprising, and many started making ice cream from home, then started selling from hand pushed carts and then pony carts. Later they became proper businesses pioneering the British ice cream industry importing foodstuffs and ingredients from their native towns and villages.

There are some fascinating books all about the history if you get chance Dan. Over the years many married into the local community, they made their own entertainment playing accordions and dancing and singing in the street. Maybe this Gary Smith is a descendant of an Italian family?"

Ancoats, Little Italy, well, well that is really interesting Sam, thanks for that, wait until I tell Billy".

Now with just the two of them in the office Shivi and Dan looked at each other as the clock on the wall hit 11.

"Love to be a fly on the wall upstairs this morning", Shivi said.

They were both thinking the same thing, trying to imagine why after all these years Collier and Bartosz had decided to come back to Manchester and speak to the Police.

To take his mind of things Dan started to go through everything he had about the apparent investment scam and how it could have started.

His mind kept going back to the common fact that this Professor Clifford had been a regular speaker at the London seminars, and he was almost certain that this is where Holroyd and Peter the Scotland Yard accountant would have likely met. Maybe if we could find the professor, he may just be able to confirm this and identify other regular attendees.

"Shivi, do me a favour and see if you can find an address for Professor James Clifford, he was a Professor of Economics at Oxford University, so he probably lives in that general locality.

And check the rough date again when the Holroyd and Dorsey emails started to get threatening, and communication suddenly stopped from this mystery man Zac Gold, if he ever existed".

According to the professor's own book he is the son of Jewish German immigrants who escaped the Nazi atrocities. He writes that his father was his inspiration in life to adapt and change. Clifford certainly doesn't sound like a Jewish German sounding surname, so how did the professors name change come about he wondered.

"Shivi, also see if you can find any record of a birth certificate for this Professor James Clifford, his book says that he was born in 1947 in London, maybe he was adopted".

"James Clifford, born 1947 in London? I'm on it Dan".

The Bartosz and Collier interviews upstairs were clearly going to be a long job as Dan and Shivi occasionally glanced at the office clock.

Dan decided to lay out a summary of what they had discovered so far about the Dorsey connection to the investment scam and how threatening emails made may have led to the photographer's murder, despite their instructions from above not to investigate this area at all.

After all Dorsey had transferred around 1 million into Zac Gold's account and the mystery man had suddenly disappeared along with the money, he had clearly fallen for the scam and was threatening revenge. What if this Zac Gold did exist and hired a hit man to get rid of Dorsey, that would be motive for murder surely.

"Dan I've found an old address for a J Clifford, actually not many Clifford's listed in the Oxford area, sounds very grand, it's in a village close to Oxford called Kingston Bagpuize. The information is from a while back so no guarantee it's him but there is a phone number listed, worth a try, eh?".

"Yep, worth a try Shivi, thanks, give me the details".

"Well at least the number is ringing out, that's a good sign" Dan said.

It continued to ring out for quite a while before an out of breath male voice answered, *"Hanover House".*

Dan said, "*Oh, I wonder if you can help me, I am trying to get in touch with Professor James Clifford, do I have the right address?".*

The lengthy answer that followed left Dan listening in complete silence with expressions of eye-opening surprise glances over at Shivi.

The conversation lasted a good 20 minutes with Dan scribbling away on a note pad and Shivi now straining over Dan's shoulder to try to see what he was writing.

When he finally put the phone down Dan said, *"Go and get us some strong coffee Shivi, we've definitely got the right address, but things are not as straight forward as I thought".*

While Shivi was away, the phone rang, it was Billy. *"It's going to be a long day Dan, they brought their solicitor with them, we are having a rest break so everyone can get some lunch. There is so much to tell you, you will get a surprise for sure, got to go now, let's meet up at the Crown & Anchor tonight and I'll tell you all about it".*

And have I've got a few things to tell you Dan thought, and then also decided it may be best not to tell Shivi the full story before he had discussed it with Billy.

The man had politely apologised for the delay in answering the phone saying that he had been outside working on the front lawn.

Dan said that he was doing some research on Professor Clifford's interesting career and was hoping to see if he could speak to him, adding that he had already read the professor's book "Change".

The out of breath man said that he is the caretaker at the house and whilst confirming this was the correct address of Professor Clifford, he half chuckled and said that it was unlikely he would be able to speak to him.

Dan then asked if perhaps the caretaker would be happy to answer a few questions himself, and as if glad of the opportunity to speak to someone, the man agreed, said his name was Fairclough, and this is what Fairclough said:

"I now live alone at the house ensuring the property is to be kept adequately maintained until it will ultimately have to be sold.

I have been an employee of the professor's father, the late Mr Clifford at Hanover House for many years and have known James since he was quite young.

Mr Clifford senior was a clever man. He left Germany when Hitler's Nazi party was growing, and Jews were beginning to be targeted. He had come from a quite well-off family which enabled him and his wife Rebecca to move to America where they settled in New York, and he became an investor in the stock market.

The couple then moved to London where Mr Clifford invested in a few properties before buying the grand house in our village close to Oxford as he always wanted his son James to have the best education money could buy and Oxford University had been the ambition for their only son and heir.

The house was renamed Hanover House after the part of Germany they came from.

When James's father died after a very short illness around ten years ago, it hit James hard, who by then was a respected Professor of Economics at Oxford University.

At the time there was also a housemaid and a cook living in quarters of the house along with myself looking after the upkeep of the house and the quite large surrounding garden areas.

After a short while, James started acting a little strangely which was noticeable not only to me but also the cook and maid. James began to smoke his father's old pipe, when he had never even smoked a cigarette before.

James's mother Hannah had passed away some years earlier and bachelor James was now master of the house and his father had always been his hero and role model.

Matters worsened when James started using his father's old study and would spend most evenings alone apparently working on his computer.

Then he started calling the maid Rebecca, his mother's name, and became agitated when she didn't respond. He was clearly unwell, and the family doctor was called and said it was likely the sudden shock of losing his father that had brought on his problems.

His odd behaviour had also manifested itself at work and the university gave him an enforced period of leave hoping that a break and medication would help, but quite the opposite was the case as at home he was beginning to almost take on his father's persona and the long serving loyal maid quit, shortly followed by the cook.

The doctor by now realised that James was certainly suffering from not only Dementia, but deeper issues and later referred him to a psychiatrist who diagnosed a form of schizophrenia, confirming that James now definitely had split personalities.

To summarise Mr Nichols, sadly James is now a permanent resident in a private rest home being cared for by professionals. I have only been to visit him once and he didn't even recognise me, the experience was so upsetting that I have never been since.

I suppose you could try to speak to him at Leafy View Manor, it's just on the outskirts of Oxford city centre. The staff told me that James is happy in his own world and sometimes likes to give talks to other patients adopting a different name. This personality imagination apparently was not unusual with some of the patients, they told me one chap is convinced he is Winston Churchill and walks in the grounds wearing a bowler hat and smoking a cigar.

I remember Mr Clifford senior once telling me that when they came to

London and his wife became pregnant, he decided to adopt a new family surname name to start their new life.

I will always remember, he told me he chose the name Clifford as he said it was an old Saxon name meaning ford by the cliff and it seemed appropriate because in Germany, he had been brought up in a hilly area at the foot of which was a river crossing.

Whilst he was in New York, his birth name Zacharias Golberg was readily accepted particularly in his profession dealing in the stock market where his work colleagues always called him Zac Gold.

There was a deadly silence as Dan heard what Fairclough had just said.

"Are you still there Mr Nichols?"

"Yes, I'm still hear, did you just say James's father was known as Zac Gold" Dan said.

"Yes, that's right Mr Nichols, in the doctor's own words, James had become his father in his mixed-up mind, and even adopted his name".

Dan was again silent.

"Are you still there Mr Nichols?

"Sorry, yes, thank you so much for speaking to me Mr Fairclough", Dan finally said and put the phone down still in a sort of trance.

CHAPTER 39

Dan was on his second beer and had been constantly looking at his watch by the time Billy arrived.

"You look knackered Billy, what took you so long, I got our beers in earlier but I'm already halfway into yours, it was going flat", Dan said.

"Well go and get us another with a whisky chaser as well" Billy said handing Dan a twenty-pound note and now a huge grin on his face.

"These drinks are on DI Morris, our work is done Danny boy, today would you believe we finally discovered who murdered Arnold Frederick Dorsey.

Dan certainly wasn't expecting that and was all geared up to tell Billy what he had found out himself over the day, but this would have to wait.

Over the next hour, helped along by a few drinks Billy explained what had surprisingly been revealed in the presence of a lawyer.

"I told you they turned up with their lawyer didn't I, well it was strange, there was another man with them as well who we assumed was a second lawyer, maybe one to represent them both individually.

The first man identified himself as Mr Eastham a solicitor from a local law firm here in Manchester and confirmed that he was here to represent both Mr and Mrs Bartosz explaining that Mr Bartosz was formerly named Victor Collier and that he had legally changed his name whilst in London and the couple were legally married. He produced the full documentation to confirm all this.

"Well, who was the second man then", Dan said.

"The solicitor said the other man was Mr Gustaw Wojcik who was also his client and who he would also be representing today.

"His client? I don't get that Billy, I'm confused already".

"We were totally confused as well, and DI Morris explained that the purpose of today's visit was to interview Mr and Mrs Bartosz in connection with a specific unsolved case they were investigating and that his other client Mr Wojcik could wait in another room until they had finished.

The solicitor said he was fully aware of the case being investigated and added that Mr Wojcik also wished to speak to them regarding this same matter. DI Morris said that we would deal with that later.

We then interviewed the now Mr and Mrs Bartosz individually in the presence of their legal representative Mr Eastham which was to be honest straight forward and they had left Manchester as the Dorsey matter was so upsetting and they knew nothing of relevance about the murder.

The later interview of Gustaw Wojcik however was the real eye opener.

When Sam had been to see Krystna Bartosz in London and said she would need to give a formal Police statement here in Manchester, she had called Gustaw Wojcik in Manchester who she said was a long-standing friend of many years from when she lived here, simply to ask him if he knew of a solicitor who could be present.

"So, why did this fella Wojcik come in as well and feel he had to have his solicitor with him Billy".

Billy was in full flow by now, clearly enjoying revealing the full story and said in his best Noel Coward voice, *"Patience my dear boy, patience, wait to be surprised.*

Do you remember ages ago; I went to the address we had for Bartosz on her statement confirming Collier's version that the two were together in her Manchester flat at the time of the murder.

Bartosz had long gone but I did speak to a tenant called Carol who remembered her, and confirmed she had a regular chap called Victor who was very often seen there at the flat.

This Carol also told me that Bartosz gave birth to a little girl called Hanna. She also said that the owner of the flats, a man called Gus was also a regular caller at her flat.

It was generally felt that Victor was the father, but there was gossip that Gus himself could be, even though he was so much older and assumed to be married, as he allowed Bartosz and baby Hanna to stay in the flat long after most of the other tenants had left.

Wait for this Danny boy, it now turns out that the landlord Gus was a man called Wojcik, Gustaw Wojcik. As the name suggests he is also Polish.

When Bartosz's mother Zofia came to England from Krakow as a young woman to study and to start a new life, she was befriended by some within the small Polish community here in Manchester and that is when she met up with Gustaw Wojcik.

She needed somewhere to stay and Wojcik, known as Gus, found a place for her to live and became a true friend keeping a caring eye on her welfare particularly after Zofia became pregnant and gave birth to Krystna.

Some within the community looked upon Wojcik as a sort of "Mister Fix-it", a religious God-fearing man who would help those in need, however some he had crossed swords with saw him more of a mafia like "Godfather figure".

And listen to this Dan, he also owned a local taxi company, the very same taxi firm that Brenda Barnes husband Tom had worked for, and he had learned from Tom what was happening at Dorsey's supposed gentlemen's cultural evening club, and how it had caused Tom and Brenda's marriage split, and Tom's subsequent breakdown and decision to leave Manchester. Gustaw Wojcik had never even met Dorsey, but he already despised him, but then things got much worse".

"Hang on, are you telling me that Wojcik is the killer Billy, surely just knowing the sad news of one of his drivers wouldn't be enough motive to commit murder. Is this Wojcik a big fella?".

"As it happens, yes he is Dan, a big strapping fella who will be in his late-fifties I would guess, why".

"Well, we know that the murderer must have been a big strong man to overcome and beat and strangle Dorsey the way he did, so I guess he would have the means, and who knows possibly the opportunity, but motive? surely not". Dan said.

"As I said, then things got worse. What finally made him make the decision that Dorsey had to go was revealed in what was Wojcik's recorded under caution confession. He said he knew it was time for Dorsey to face justice in the form of retribution when he discovered the following.

Krystna's little daughter Hanna loved drawing and was encouraged to do so by Wojcik who had given her a little sketch pad and pencil which she always had with her.

For the short period that Krystna had worked as a cleaner at Dorsey's studio she had to take Hanna with her. Hanna would play in a small room making drawings of the things around her.

Wojcik knew Krystna had found a job where she could take little Hanna with her, but didn't know it was at Dorsey's studio. Victor had approached Dorsey to see if it was possible and Dorsey, remembering her from the Greek Mythology classes knew she was an attractive shapely young woman and agreed.

Each time Wojcik visited at their flat, he would spend a little time with little Hanna and look at her sketch pad. She was very good for such a young age and sketched flowers and cats and trees and happy things. He had shown her how to draw her own hand by tracing the pencil around her fingers. Despite the earlier rumours, Wojcik had never married and by now he considered Krystna and Hanna as family.

On his last visit, he noticed that Hanna had started drawing a keyhole with images that she could see through into another room. When he asked about them, she said the door was locked, but he didn't know which door or what she was talking about. One image showed Hanna's own eye in the keyhole.

He was surprised and confused at some of the other images she had drawn, which if he interpreted them right, was clearly not what he considered a child should see.

He showed the sketches to Krystna and asked what they could mean, but she admitted she had not even noticed these recent ones as Hanna was always drawing things around her every day.

One of the keyhole images looked as though it could be a lady showing her body posing. It also showed a black cat on the floor drinking out of a bowl and that it when Krystna realised it was Dorsey's studio.

When she told Wojcik that her cleaning job was at Dorsey's studio, he hit the roof. Knowing what had happened to his taxi driver Tom, he immediately told Krystna she was not to ever step foot in Dorsey's place again, furthermore he arranged for her to get away from Manchester and arranged a flat in the London area where she and Hanna could stay.

"But what about Collier" Dan said, *"what did he do?"*

Billy was in full flow by now, clearly enjoying revealing the full story.

By this time, Wojcik was aware that Victor Collier was Hanna's father, and he was quite happy with that as he knew Collier was a good honest young man and suggested he also should go with Krystna and the child, however he decided to stay with his mother a while longer. She didn't even know Victor had a young daughter and he had kept it secret from her and didn't really know how he could tell her, plus he had already been summoned to attend Dorsey's postmortem identification.

As we know in the event Collier didn't tell his mother, and simply left Manchester and disappeared off the radar shortly after the murder and his mother never even knew where he had gone.

We now know that Victor Collier did join Krystna Bartosz in London. He changed his name to Bartosz and they were married.

Knowing what had gone on in Dorsey's studio, and then his sudden murder they were scared and wanted to distance themselves from the whole situation.

"Did Wojcik say how he managed to get into the studio to see Dorsey after it had closed for the day, and what about the anonymous snuff box and tooth Billy?".

His hatred for Dorsey was now such that he planned his demise.

What he told us was that he contacted Dorsey with a made-up story to say he had a model agency and wanted to see if the studio was suitable to shoot some promotional material for which he would pay well and if so, it would be a regular thing.

Dorsey jumped at the chance and that is how he let him in to the studio.

As for the anonymous parcel with the snuff box and tooth etc. Wojcik was a religious man and had read his bible and felt that as little Hanna's eye had been violated, he said, "she had seen what she had seen, and couldn't just un-see these images" and the appropriate retribution should be "an eye for an eye, and a tooth for a tooth". So, guess what Danny boy, you were spot with that.

So why has it taken so long for him to own up and confess Billy?

He says over these years he had become more aware of his faith and had spent more time at church and had started feeling the strong pangs of guilt for what he had done. He had been to confession to seek help and asked the Priest, "Is it a sin to right a wrong by committing another sin Father". The Priest said he should read his bible saying, "Perdition".

When he read the bible again, it was clear that he would be on his pathway to perdition, in a state of eternal punishment when he passes after death unless he repents his sin.

When he saw the public appeal for information into Dorsey's murder, that is when he sent the snuff box and tooth anonymously to the Police when he was visiting London, he said it made him feel at least halfway to owning up to the sin he had committed and repenting.

It was only when he got the call from Krystna Bartosz a few days ago to say that Police had located her and that she had to come in to be interviewed that he felt it would be a further sin if he didn't explain that his act was a lone act, and neither Krystna nor Victor ever knew anything about it.

"Do they know now?", Dan said.

"No, they were free to go before we interviewed Wojcik, and there are some legal processes to go through before his confession is looked at by the CPS. They could be on their way back to London by now, probably relieved that they can get on with their open lives from here on", Billy said.

"Gustaw Wojcik eh? who would have thought, he was never even on the radar all these years, sounds like he is a pretty mixed-up fella to me", Dan said.

CHAPTER 40

Dan was last to arrive at the office the next morning where the atmosphere was upbeat with DI Morris present, smiling and congratulating the team on their success before patting Dan on the back as he left the room with a large smile on his face and probably heading for a vanilla slice.

After this latest success Dan was still thinking on the Zac Gold issue and just couldn't get it off his mind, and with everything going on he hadn't even had chance to tell Billy about it. Coming face to face with DI Morris he was now thinking how on earth they would be able to pass this information to him and DCI Geoff Gill, when they had blatantly disobeyed their order not to investigate that matter.

In his military days the term Court Marshal came to mind. and he couldn't hide the concern on his face.

"What's up with you Dan, you look like you've just had Hitler's gas bill? you should be pleased" Billy said.

"Well, it was just the other matter of the investment scam business and this Zac Gold, I've not had chance to tell you Billy."

"It will have to wait Dan, I'm off to Angus's funeral, you can tell me later", Billy said grabbing his coat.

"And I had a call from Victor Collier's mother first thing, so I'm off to see her now," Sam said as she left at the same time as Billy.

Dan looked over at Shivi, who just shrugged his shoulders as if to say, what do we do now?

Later, on his return to the office Billy explained that the funeral had been a low-key affair with just Billy, Polish Joe, the two other railway arch occupants and the couple of men from the local Council department who had arranged the cremation.

Billy had persuaded Baldy Gary to be there and play a couple of old Scottish shanties on Angus's concertina, and the final view of the coffin as the curtains closed had Angus's old Long John Silver type wooden crutch laid on top, so they were still together at the very end.

A sad day when a soldier who had lost a leg fighting for his country and who had also lost the battle to recover from the trauma and survive back home in peacetime.

On the upside, the highlighting of Angus's sad lifestyle had resulted in a Council decision to find hostel accommodation for Polish Joe and the other two and clear out the arches and convert them into two separate sections which could be let off for business use as secure storage units or a small car repair workshop.

"Now this Zac Gold business Billy", Dan said, but before he had chance to say another word Sam came through the door with a huge grin on her face and said, *"what a satisfying morning I've had", I went to see Rose Collier who greeted me like a long-lost friend with tears of joy in her eyes. I've been like a social worker today"*

Without stopping for breath, she relayed the conversation she had had with Rose Collier. The son she had not seen for all these years had turned up on her doorstep along with Krystna Bartosz and she learned that not only did she have a daughter in law, but Rose was a grandmother. She was over the moon and had already been making plans to visit them and her granddaughter Hanna in London.

Sam went on to say that in view of the confession by Gustaw Wojcik she had also paid a visit to Brenda Barnes to inform her that a man had been arrested for the murder of Dorsey.

She had cleared this with DI Morris first as it was soon to be released to the press that an unnamed man was in custody. The poor woman had lived all these years mentally torturing herself that her husband Tom had murdered Dorsey because of her foolish actions.

"A satisfying day all around then eh", Sam said.

"And it's been a long day as well", Billy said looking at the clock. *"We have a busy day tomorrow preparing all our case files for the CPS, so see you all tomorrow".*

"Fancy a quick beer on the way home Billy?" Dan said, thinking I've got to tell him about Zac Gold.

In the comfort of the Crown & Anchor the success in the Dorsey murder case was cause for a whisky as the two pals raised their glasses.

"Case closed then eh Danny boy, Mike Morris and DCI Geoff Gill are really chuffed".

"But that still leaves us with the other business, what do we do about the Zac Gold information Billy?".

"What do you mean, what do we do, we don't have to do anything Dan, we thought there may just be a connection with Dorsey's murder, but now we know there wasn't, so we don't even have to mention it, anyway the search for the Met's missing money is being dealt with by Scotland Yard's financial IT experts.

"But I've found Zac Gold Billy, he does exist and is alive and well, maybe not that well, but he's alive and I know where he is, and I know where his computer will be, which I am guessing is where the key to all the stolen money can be found and hopefully even recovered, we've got to tell the boss".

"What, when did all this happen and why on earth didn't you tell me?"

"I have been trying to tell you all day Billy but there has been so much going on, but what do we do about it now.

"Well, if you've found him probably the Scotland Yard top dogs will have found him, so best say nothing".

"But they won't have found him Billy, I'm sure, we know the email address for Gold ceased years ago and his bank at that time will have been emptied and transferred elsewhere. Listen I know who he is, and where he now is at this moment, we've got to tell the boss".

Over the next hour helped along with a few more drinks, Dan explained how his simple general interest in Professor J. Clifford unfolded and discovered this unexpected and surprising information.

"Professor Clifford is Zac Gold; this is all hard to take in Dan, but listen, I still think we were justified in looking at Holroyd's laptop stuff as it did show threats to Zac Gold from Dorsey if his multi-million-pound investment wasn't paid within a week, which could have sparked Gold to maybe hire a hit man and get rid of Dorsey first, **he** *may have had friends in high places as well, who knows".*

Billy then laughed and said, *"From what you have told me, Zac Gold does have one very influential friend, it's not everyone who lives in the same house as Winston Churchill eh?".*

"So where is his computer which you think will hold information on bank details where his ill-gotten money can be found?".

"It's got to be in the professor's fathers' studio at Hanover House Billy. The room has been kept locked since he was diagnosed with dementia and his split personally stuff, but how do we pass all this on upstairs without admitting we disobeyed their direct orders?".

"What can they do Danny boy, sack us? we've finished our role anyway. We were tasked to review the cold case, and we have done, and with a result. Mike Morris is on a high now, as you know he only agreed to delay his retirement to take on this last job, so I don't want to ruin his day, he is really looking forward to finally retiring.

" Listen, I know the system Dan, if they find out we have deliberately gone against orders, upstairs will be looking for someone to blame and that will likely be our immediate superior officers, and that means Mike and DCI Geoff Gill will get it in the neck and we can't let that happen".

"You are right Billy, let's just let it go and say nothing and just hope like you say, the Scotland Yard special team come to the same conclusion after their own in-depth work".

CHAPTER 41

Dan met up with Paula again on Sunday and drove out to a country pub for lunch. Neither had been to this place before and it felt cosy with a real log fire burning providing a welcoming atmosphere.

Over lunch and a nice glass of wine Dan remembered Paula's reference to Oxford and the fact that she had never been there before, and he suggested that perhaps they could take a trip there in the future saying that the city was steeped in history with so much to see. Paula raised her glass, smiled and said, *"I would really look forward to that Dan".*

She started asking Dan about his military days in the Intelligence Corps, but old habits die hard and even now he still had this built-in reaction to try to change the subject as it was always the practice to say as little as possible.

He did this by simply saying he had also been lucky to have seen many places around the world just like she had, then switched the conversation by asking Paula what it was like being a military wife and living in the community of a camp base.

She said she had been surprised how much she had enjoyed the comradery of the other wives and had made many friends. There always seemed to be something going on, keep fit and other activity facilities etc. She said she particularly looked forward to what was a common tradition of having what they called a "Safari Supper" where we would visit each other's homes, starting the meal at the first home, then moving on to the next home for the second course and so on, until finishing supper at the last house.

Dan said that in his Sunday School days he remembered this same idea being called a "Jacob's Join" by his parents.

By now it was common knowledge that a person had been arrested and charged with Dorsey's murder and Paula asked Dan if he was pleased it was all over, and that his time working at the station had now come to an end.

"Not quite finished yet Paula, we still have a few days of tidying up to do

and pass everything on to the CPS. I suppose I will be glad in one way; this wasn't my plan when I finished work and came back here to retire and enjoy the autumn years if you know what I mean, but I have to say I have enjoyed the challenge of the job, and I will certainly miss the other members of our close knit little team".

"What will you do then Dan, still see Billy I'm sure, but what about the things you originally planned to do?

"To be completely honest with you Paula, I have been thinking about that over the past few days, originally, I was going to enjoy reading and listening to my music in the quiet comfort of my place, as if every day could be like a leisurely Sunday. Having long walks in the countryside, going into a local pub and reading a newspaper or doing the crossword, simple things.

"Obviously I will still spend time with Billy, who I know will go straight back into his old lifestyle, especially his open mike nights at the Golden Ball and will still have his ear to the ground about what's going on in what he still calls "his old patch" from his PC days.

I've been surprised just how well he is still respected and has retained so many of his old contacts, I know he can come across a bit full on sometimes, but really he's just a big old softie who can't stand people being ripped off or taken advantage of, If he gets a bee in his bonnet, it wouldn't surprise me if he still has the impulse to try to stick his nose in and try to solve injustices he hears about. Providing he doesn't want to drag me along, eh?". Dan said.

"From what I have heard I suspect you wouldn't need too much persuading to go along with him Dan" Paula said as they headed out of the pub onto the car park.

As they approached the car somebody shouted, *"hey Dan"* and when they looked round Dan said, *"Oh it's Simon and Jean, they must have been in the pub in the other room, I hadn't noticed them".*

The couple came over and Dan said, *"It's good to see you, this is Paula, Paula meet my neighbours from the apartments Simon and Jean".*

After exchanging niceties Simon said, *"We haven't really seen you for ages Dan, if you are heading home, why not come back to ours for a coffee and catch up".*

Dan looked at Paula for a reaction and was surprised when she said, *"That would be really nice wouldn't it Dan, thank you".*

On the drive back Dan explained that Simon was a retired solicitor, and he and Jean lived in the top floor sort of penthouse apartment. He explained that they were a lovely couple, and Simon had assisted him when he first decided to buy his apartment.

"It's a beautiful place you have here Jean", Paula said as they had coffee in the lounge.

"Now then Dan, I hear you have been working with Billy in the cold case review team at the station, we guessed you were doing some kind of work as we've hardly seen you over the past months. I still occasionally socialise with a couple of solicitors I know, and they mentioned it, and a man has been arrested and charged with the murder of that photographer, the team must have done a good job", Simon said.

"Let me show you around the rest of the apartment Paula while the men are talking shop", Jean said.

"I really enjoyed today, and it was so nice to meet Simon and Jean, they seem really nice", Paula said on the drive back to her place.

"Jean was showing me some photographs of their son Trevor, and she told me how you had helped through your old military contacts when the plane Trevor was travelling in went missing in the Dominican Republic and how they thought they had lost him, I didn't know you worked in London for a while after finishing in the army, so you actually retired twice by the time you came back to Manchester".

"Yes, I went to work for my old captain who runs a private security and detective agency, it at least gave me time to get used to living in civi street I suppose. Yes, that was a terrible time for Simon and Jean, but luckily all turned out well in the end and I did meet up with Trevor after he got back to the UK", Dan replied.

"Well, I guess we won't be bumping into each other at work from next week onwards will we Dan, maybe this will be third time lucky retirement, eh?

Dan dropped her off right at her door after a kiss in the car and Paula waived him off blowing another kiss. Dan felt good

CHAPTER 42

"*So, what happens now?*", Shivi said as all the files, statements and documented notes were being gathered and boxed up to pass to the Crown Prosecution Service.

"The CPS office will prepare the case for trial to be heard at Crown Court", Sam said.

"Well, he's confessed and pleaded guilty so the trial shouldn't take long should it", Shivi said.

"Justice has to be seen to be done dear boy" Billy piped up in his posh Noel Coward voice without looking up from what he was doing.

"Yeh, but murder's murder isn't it", Shivi replied.

"It's not quite as simple as that" Sam said. *"The court will hear all the evidence which will seek to determine the classification of the murder, first degree murder, second degree with no premeditation, manslaughter, diminished responsibility, self-defence even who knows.*

Wojcik will be represented, everyone is entitled to a defence, his legal team will be looking at any mitigation, I suppose they could insist on a medical examination to assess whether he was mentally fit to plea. All this will influence the jury, and on the Judge's final sentence, Wojcik may even be persuaded to change his plea.

All those issues could be considered, anyway that's for a jury to decide and for the Judge to pass an appropriate sentence".

"We did our bit Shivi, gathering the evidence, so job done eh" Dan said just as the door opened and DI Morris and DCI Gill came in with smiles on their faces.

"We both wanted to congratulate the team, and here's a letter from the Chief Constable as well, expressing his thanks for your hard work and determination in getting a result" DCI Gill said.

"And drinks on me, see you all in the Bull later eh" Mike Morris beamed.

It was quiet in the Bull, but it was early doors and mid-week with just a few faces from the station stood chatting at the bar. Mike took out a few folded-up notes from his wallet and said, "You go and get the drinks in Billy, while we will get a table over there away from any ear wiggers".

Looks like these notes haven't seen the light of day for a while Billy mumbled to himself as he unfolded the money and crossed to the bar. He immediately spotted smarmy Eddie Frost from the local gazette trying to get into conversation with some of the fellas at the far end of the bar.

Mike was still enjoying things and was chatting away with the others when Billy brought the drinks on a tray. *"Scotch and chaser for you and me Mike, G and T for Sam and half a beer for you two lightweights"*, Billy said passing the final drinks to Shivi and Dan.

"Cheers everyone", Mike said as he downed his whisky in one, with Billy not far behind. The others raised their glasses and Billy said *"Cheers, and here's to your well-deserved retirement Mike, you finally made it".*

"Well not quite yet Billy, Mike said, *"we still have to see this to the end and although the CPS don't think it's likely any of you will be called to give evidence at the trial, we will all have to make ourselves available in case we are called".*

I'm' going to get us another snifter Mike, whether you like it or not, what about you lot?".

"Just another half for me Billy" Dan said.

"Not for me Billy, I will have to be getting on" Sam said. *"Me too Shivi joined in, but thanks anyway, must be going".*

When Mike went to the gents and it was now just Billy and Dan, Billy leaned over and said, *"I've got an idea Dan, after you've finished your drink, you shoot off so I can speak to Mike alone, I'll explain later and see you in the office tomorrow".*

Dan finished his half and said, *"Well, I'm off as well now, so thanks for the drinks Mike, see you tomorrow Billy".*

"Just the two of us now Mike eh, Billy said, *"like old times, where did the years go? I remember my spell in CID with you, we had some laughs back in those days, didn't we?"*

Mike finished the last drop of his drink, leaned back in his chair for a second in deep thought and said, *"We sure did, let's have another scotch".*

"I'll get these", Billy said

Mike was still trying to remember the names of some of the characters they had encountered when Billy got back.

"Yep, some happy days eh Mike. You know that me and Dan go back even way further to school days. I know he's a bit of a nerd, always has his nose in a book and looking up historical facts. He doesn't think like a Policeman, but he is a deep thinker even if it's sometimes thinking outside the box.

He always wants us to have a "What If" session and sometimes goes off at a tangent. I'll give you a perfect example, this will make you laugh, you know this Zac Gold business".

Mike looked around and said, *"Keep your voice down".*

Billy moved over right next to Mike and leaned closer.

CHAPTER 43

Dan had been home for about an hour and was still wondering why Billy had wanted to speak to Mike Morris alone. What was he up to, wouldn't be surprised if he was trying to talk Mike into having another retirement do at the Golden Ball after his last short lived one.

Ah well an early night tonight, but not before a glass of scotch.

As he sat back in his chair he started pondering on Paula's question as to what he was going to do once the trial was over. What about Sam and Shivi?

Sam will just return to her normal CID duties, she is a good Detective Constable, but what about Shivi, back to Police College? The experience must have been a great move forward for him and as far as Dan and Billy were concerned, he was very competent as their IT researcher.

Dan chuckled to himself remembering back to when Shivi first arrived at the office and his "workstation" description where all his IT equipment was to be set up, and then Billy forever calling his DJ deck as his workstation.

So, what for Dan himself? lazy days relaxing catching up on his reading and crossword puzzle solving, listening to his music, maybe even that trip to Oxford he had promised Paula. One more tot of scotch before his eyes started going.

The first chance he got Billy on his own Dan said, *"What was this chatting privately with the boss in the Bull all about last night?"*

"I'd been thinking about the Zac Gold business again Dan, you know when I said Mike would be the one who would get the blame if the powers that be found out we had disobeyed orders, well what if Mike discovered who Gold is, then surely it figures he would equally personally get the credit as well wouldn't it?".

"What exactly are you getting at Billy" Dan said looking a bit perplexed.

"Look, you eventually got to the bottom of it by joining up all the dots, so what if we were to provide Mike with just some of the starting dots, bits

of the jigsaw, I'm pretty sure he would pass that info up the line and the Scotland Yard brains would work it out as well.

Without realising it, it would mean that Mike had been instrumental in solving the puzzle and who knows even lead to locating the Met's stolen money and recovering it. That would be a feather in his cap and a win- win situation wouldn't it."

"But how can we do that Sherlock" Dan said.

Billy looked a bit sheepish and eventually said, *"I've already done it Dan".*

"What on earth have you said to him Billy?"

"Well, in a way, I suppose I sort of blamed it on you Dan, but calm down, his order was not to do any research at all re this Zac Gold, and you didn't. Out of curiosity and in your own time you simply looked at the background of a man who was regular speaker at the special seminars in London.

To his credit Mike always was a good listener, admittedly a few shots of scotch may have made him a bit more receptive in the Bull last night. Remember he already knew we had briefly seen the stuff on Holroyd's laptop before it was all quickly confiscated, so this little bit of chat didn't totally surprise him I guess"

Billy then told Dan exactly what he had said to Mike Morris, all about the professor's book and the fact that it mentioned that his father was German who as a Jew had fled when the Hitler regime was on the rise and went to America, then had changed his family name when he came to the UK from the USA. Then crucially the fact that the father's original name was Zacharias Goldberg, and I said that you being you put two and two together and got five saying "What If" this professor shortened the name to Zac Gold and adopted the name himself.

He had told Mike about Dan's What If sessions and passion for reading and doing crosswords, particularly cryptic clues, and that's when he said Dan had come up with this novel idea, or What If there was a connection that would lead to the illusive Zac Gold. Mike had just laughed and said, "who is this professor then Billy?"

I pretended not to remember at first then said, I think his name is Clifford, yes that's it, Professor James Clifford, then we just laughed again and finished our drinks and our walk down memory lane.

"Oh, so you told him I was a nerd eh, well thanks for that Billy. What happens now then Sherlock?"

"Nothing Watson dear friend, we just sit back, we have all done our bit and if I know Mike he will be looking at the mad Professors book himself and won't be able to resist passing on the starting dot clues, even though he thinks it's just a wild "What If" theory of yours. Then we wait and see."

"I just hope you are right Billy.

CHAPTER 44

It was no more than a final clear up at the office, then a waiting game to hear from the CPS re the trial.

It was eerily quiet as each one of the team had been thinking about their own situation once the office was finally redundant, closed and locked up.

Shivi had been seeing more of Miranda and was hoping that could continue after his move on from the station.

Sam was due some leave and was planning a little break, it had been a while since she and husband Denis had managed to get away for a little holiday.

Billy and landlord Dougie had already planned "the grand re-opening" of the Golden Ball open mike nights. He had got the night's entertainment programme sorted out with Dougie who was in charge of booking the acts, including *Whistling Walter from Warrington* who had this unique skill of shoving two fingers in his mouth and whistling his way through the complete theme music to the movie "Watership Down", then similar leg crossing songs like "Cry me a River" and "On the Rivers of Babylon".

Dougie had reminded him that the last time Walter had performed like that they had to immediately have a fifteen-minute toilet break for the audience before the show could carry on. Walter also had the skill of impersonating a catalogue of different bird sounding squeaks and whistles.

Dougie said if Walter was to do this again, he must not ask the audience to shout out names of their favourite birds to see if he could do their call, as this had resulted in old Duncan continuously shouting *"tits"* from the back of the room, which eventually led to him being politely escorted out. Duncan was OK until he had too much to drink, which was quite often, but at the age of 87 he was harmless and most of the crowd new him as *Duncan Disorderly*.

Dougie had told me he tried to book *Strong Man Stan* from Stockport.

He said Stan could bend iron bars like they were rubber, he also claimed to be an escapologist, but unfortunately Stan was still in Strangeways doing another six months. Dougie still makes me laugh with all these names.

The silence was broken when Shivi said, *"I'll be glad when I don't have to fiddle about with this old roller blind any more"*, as he pulled it down then stood and watched for a few seconds, only to see the thing spring back up again the very instant he sat down, as if it had been watching him.

"Well, remember Shivi" Billy said, *"If it wasn't for roller blinds, it would be curtains for us all"*. Which at least caused a chuckle from the others just as DI Morris came in.

"Good to see a happy team. Just thought I would let you know that the CPS have agreed with Wojcik's lawyers to have him examined by an independent specialist psychiatrist to give an opinion as to his state of mind, and whether his original confession plea should be looked at again" Mike said. *"But before that, while he is still in custard, bloody hell Billy, you've got me saying it now, I mean in CUSTODY on remand, we need him interviewed again.*

Sam, I want you to do that, you've got a copy of his original statement, get him to go over everything again, exactly what he did to Dorsey in every detail. Are you OK with that?

"No problem boss will do" Sam replied.

"There is no doubt in anyone's mind that he committed the murder, and he clearly planned it in advance, but there is still a way to go before the CPS are ready, so it's much too early to even think about a trial date yet", Mike continued.

CHAPTER 45

When Wojcik was brought into the interview room he looked tired and dishevelled. The comfort of a Police cell had not provided him with any desire to even try to sleep.

Over the next almost full hour, Sam asked Wojcik to tell her again exactly what he had done and why he had done it, addressing him by his first name Gus, and telling him in an almost sympathetic manner that she was there simply to try to understand.

His answers were clear, and his recall of the actual event, and his years of guilt afterwards just confirmed the comments made in his original confession.

The original interview was little more than a "question and answer" session and Gus was again answering these questions in just the same basic way. Sam then decided to approach her questioning from a slightly different angle, maybe asking more detailed questions may produce more detailed answers she thought.

What he revealed during this new and different approach revealed some vital evidence that had been completely overlooked.

This new and surprising information started to unravel when Sam asked, *"Tell me again how you murdered Mr Dorsey".*

"I strangled him".

"How did you strangle him?"

"What do you mean?"

"Well, did you use a rope or some kind of ligature?"

"No, with my bare hands".

"So you strangled him with your bare hands, your bare hands?".

"Well, with my plastic gloves on".

"How did you get rid of the plastic gloves?"

"I didn't get rid of them".

"Well, what did you do with them?".

"I kept them along with Hanna's sketch pad I took from her so she wouldn't be reminded of those images she had drawn anymore. How can a child unsee what she had seen".

"Where are the gloves and sketch pad now Gus?".

"They are in a locked box at home, over the years I kept looking at them to remind me of what I had done".

"Why didn't you mention the gloves earlier?"

"Nobody asked me".

"OK Gus, is there anything else you would like to tell me? I know you explained that you are very close to Krystna and Hanna and always have been, they have been almost like family".

There was a slight hesitation and intake of breath before Gus said, "They are my family".

"Tell me what you mean, they are your family".

Sam was beginning to feel like a psychiatrist herself, but this approach was clearly working and getting through to Wojcik.

"I mean they **are** *my family, Krystna is my daughter and Hanna is my granddaughter.*

"Can you explain a little more Gus?"

"Krystna's mother Zofia and I knew each other from being children, our families had neighbouring farmland in Krakow. Years before there had been a dispute over the land borders which caused a family feud, and the two families never spoke to each other. However, Zofia and I would meet secretly and even just as teenagers fell in love.

When she was eventually able to leave home and come to England, our love was rekindled, and Zofia gave birth to our beautiful daughter Krystna. All of this was purposely kept secret from our families back in Poland and Zofia and I never married.

After Zofia sadly passed away, I naturally continued to look after my daughter and granddaughter, although neither Krystna or little Hanna ever knew of our true relationship and simply looked upon me as a caring friend. Even Krystna's birth certificate purposely records the father as

"Unknown". I saw little sense in telling Krystna all this, and to this day she doesn't know that I am her birth father, and I would appreciate it if this information would be kept in confidence, I don't want my own daughter and granddaughter to go through their lives thinking I was an evil person".

Sam was certain that Wojcik's defence team will want to emphasise this fact and present it at the trial as some semblance of mitigation to reduce the charge and sentence, but she didn't say anything.

"So, you took the sketch pad from Hanna initially to prevent her from being reminded of her experience at the studio, and later to reignite your anger, sufficient to want to make Mr Dorsey pay, is that what you are telling me Gus?"

"Yes, that is correct".

"Then afterwards, when you had strangled Dorsey, you also kept the gloves as a reminder, which later turned into your feeling of guilt. Is that what you are saying?"

"Yes, that is correct".

"You realise that we need to see the sketch pad and gloves to verify what you are telling me Gus, so where will we find them?"

"I have an antique granddaughter clock in my lounge at home. I bought it when little Hanna was born. There is a panel at the back which can be removed and there is a metal box inside the size of a shoe box. The box is locked, and the key is in the bottom left draw of my desk in the same room".

"Well, thank you for your cooperation, I think we can leave it there for now" Sam said.

The whole interview had been video recorded, and Sam couldn't wait for DI Morris's reaction.

Within the hour Wojcik's metal box had been retrieved from his house and the contents had been examined.

CHAPTER 46

The team were assembled in DI Morris's office for an updated debrief with DCI Geoff Gill taking the lead.

He explained that Mr Wojcik's box recovered from his property had indeed contained the child's sketch pad and more crucially the gloves he wore to strangle Dorsey. Forensics had now confirmed that the gloves not only had Dorsey's DNA on them but also blood splatters confirmed as Dorsey's, presumably from his removed tooth and savaged eye socket.

In the desk draw where the key to the box was found, there was also two small silver Polish snuff boxes, the same design as the one containing the tooth.

Inside the locked box along with the gloves and sketch pad there was also some formal looking documents and letters which included medical type records which appear to confirm Wojcik's claim that he is indeed the birth father of Krystna and grandfather of Hanna.

The debrief concluded with DCI Gill thanking each member of the review team personally with special praise for Sam for her enterprising interview techniques.

"Well, that's it Danny boy", Billy said as they headed back downstairs, but not before he noticed Dan straining to see if he could see Paula in the typing pool.

"For goodness' sake Dan, just go in and have a word with her".

"No, its OK Billy, I am seeing her again at the weekend.", then changing the subject said, "So all these latest revelations will now be disclosed by the CPS to Wojcik's defence team. Do you know, I feel a bit sorry for the fella, in his own way I suppose he was trying to protect his child and grandchild".

"Well, no one could blame him for doing that Dan, OK give him a gipsy's warning or a Glasgow handshake, but not murdering him, even though he thought he was following certain readings of the bible. Anyway, that's now for others to decide. Let's go and have a drink at the old Crown and Anchor eh, like old times".

"Yep, sounds like a plan to me Sherlock, make sure nobody's nicked our old HQ table".

As expected, the pub was almost empty, just a couple of old fellas playing darts in the far corner, well *trying* to play, as most of their arrows only just about hit the board let alone the numbers they were aiming for.

The barman said, *"How do lads, not seen you two in here for a while"*, as they got their drinks and headed over to their usual table.

Somehow their corner felt even more comfortable than before as the two old pals raised their glasses and said Cheers.

Dan thought for a while and finally said, *"You know, that was a nice thing you did for Angus, you know sorting out the funeral and getting Baldy Gary to play his old squeeze box at the service".*

"It still bugs me Dan when I think that some who fought for their country and still suffer the trauma of what they had witnessed, then are left to live like old Angus did. There must be so many others in the same situation, surely there should be some help for people like that.

I mean everyday you see adverts on the tele appealing for people to adopt a tiger, what the bloody hell are they supposed do with a tiger when the elephant and gorilla they adopted last week are still roaming about in their two up two down hey Danny boy, answer me that".

"Very funny Billy, but if you feel so passionate, why don't you do something about it then instead of just moaning?" Dan said.

"Like what"?

"I don't know, organise a raffle at the pub or something and raise money to help those like old Angus", Dan replied clearly fed up with Billy going on and on.

"You mean start a charity?"

"No, I was joking Billy, there will be lots of charities who deal with hardship like that, the Samaritans, the British Legion, they help former military don't they".

"I suppose you're right Dan, I'll stop moaning then and change the subject. But just had a thought though, if we did start a charity specifically for

trauma sufferers like Angus, we could call it, ***"Seek Help in Trauma"****, it would be called* ***SHIT*** *for short. Hey and suppose the Turd sees the light while he is doing his six months inside and comes out a reformed man, he could be the new ambassador for SHIT.*

"Let's change the subject ***Please****",* Dan said.

There was a little silence before Billy said, *"So, I am guessing you are getting quite close to Paula now Dan?"*

"We seem to hit it off to be honest, it's strange we share similar interests. I know she appears shy and quiet, but I guess anyone next to Eve gets little chance to appear anything else, but she isn't quiet at all and is very sharp and has a great sense of humour" Dan said.

"So, she's see's Eve even when she's at home I suppose, living almost next door, as well as at work every day, that must be tough. Is she still looking for another place Dan? What about that apartment at your place where that arsehole Kevin Carter lived, has it been taken yet?"

"As far as I know it must have been, I know the To Let sign has been taken down".

"Pity that Dan, it would have been nice, and I know the other people at your place are good neighbours. Don't tell me you hadn't thought about that, having Paula in the same apartment building"?

"I must admit, the thought had crossed my mind, but I don't know how Paula would have felt about that. Eve seems to be involved in virtually every local community activity from the Church Council and the Women's Institute".

"And probably in charge of everything eh? I wouldn't be surprised if she runs for office in the next bi election" Billy said.

"It was probably well intended when Paula first arrived and didn't know anyone, but now it's stifling her and she wants to move on, and who can blame her eh. Anyway, I've been meaning to ask you Billy, what do you call Jenny?"

"I call her Jenny, what do you call her?"

"No, I mean when you introduce her to someone for the first time, do you say, this is Jenny my girlfriend, lady friend, partner, companion? you know

what I mean".

"Oh dear, Daniel dear boy, you do fart around sometimes, just call Paula, your friend, it's nobody else's business anyway is it".

Ok, Ok, I only wondered, I'll go and get the drinks in then instead of farting around should I", Dan said.

When he got back, Billy was in deep thought and said, *"With you mentioning Eve, it reminded me of her brother Peter Knight at school. Do you remember another lad who was called Alfred, but nobody called him that, Just Alf, do you remember Dan"?*

"Oh no, not again Billy, NO I don't remember Alf, but no doubt you are about to remind me".

His surname was Hartigan, well he got in trouble one day at playtime, this female teacher was on playground duty and Alf sneaked up right behind her and blew a loud raspberry on the back of his hand, do you remember, everyone bust out laughing?"

"No' I don't remember but get to the point Billy".

"Well, this teacher turned around grabbed him by the ear and said what's you name boy, what have you got to say for yourself, and he said, **Alf Hartigan Miss**, *and everyone started laughing again. She said I suppose you think that's funny then led him off to see the headmaster.*

Everyone started laughing again and blowing raspberries on the back of their hands as she took poor Alf inside. Dan just frowned, waiting for something else and said, *Well?"*

"Don't you get it Dan, Alf Hartigan, ***I'll fart again".***

"You really do remember the weirdest things Billy, but I'll tell you what I do remember though, we used to look for funny book titles and authors like, The Haunted House by Hugo First."

"Yea we did, didn't we Dan, The Dangerous Cliff by Eileen Dover.

"The Unhappy Shopper by Mona Lott" Dan said.

After a little pause when both were obviously trying to think of other books, Dan finally said, *"Anyway, enough of this nonsense, how's the planning going for your next Open Mike Night, not long now, eh?".*

When Billy told him about the acts Dougie had lined up, including Whistling Walter, Dan laughed and said, *"Maybe Alf Hartigan expanded his repertoire into adulthood, and he could do a turn as well".*

"I'll have to tell that one to Dougie, anyway I think we should call it a night Dan. Can you believe it's the final day at the office tomorrow, final clear up and hand our ID cards in eh".

"Well, I've got to say it's been an interesting time Billy, these last months have certainly opened my eyes to how things work in the Police force, so much different to my army career. I suspect most in the station will have looked at us as a bit of an odd mix for a cold case team".

"Maybe they did, but remember Danny boy, we still got a result didn't we. Anyway, did you enjoy the experience?"

"I did, and I have to confess, meeting and working with Shivi and Sam each day, and with Mike Morris has been something I will never forget, and not forgetting you of course", Dan replied with a broad grin.

As they left the pub and started going their separate ways home Dan heard, *"Six Months in the Saddle by Major Bumsore".*

He didn't even turn around, just laughed and waived his hand behind him.

CHAPTER 47

Shivi was fiddling about behind his workstation and said, *"I suppose some of the lads will be back to dismantle all this lot soon then eh?"*

"That will be tickety boo then wont it" Billy said smiling over at Dan.

"Has the boss given any indication of where you will go next Shivi", Sam asked.

"No, nothing, what about you Sam".

"Before I was seconded to join your lot, I was scheduled to start a spell of attending some of the local schools to give a talk to the pupils on what they should be looking for within their own community which could show signs that drug pushing was happening and what they should do about it. I am guessing that I will be back on that agenda, but I am due a few days leave".

Has the boss said anything to you Billy"? Sam said.

"Not really, only that we are to take the rest of the week off and he will update you two then, in the meantime we have to hand in our ID cards Dan".

"A bit sad really, our final day" Sam said, "But cheer up lads, I've brought some vanilla slices in to share at coffee time, even one for DI Morris if we see him".

"Do you know Sam, talking about you giving a talk in schools, I remember that happening at my school, there was this PC, he was Asian, I can't remember his name, but he was brilliant, he was funny and encouraged the class to ask questions, and he asked questions back. I am pretty sure that his influence played a big part in me wanting to join the Police", Shivi said.

"Well, I'm glad he did Shivi, and I will take on board what you said, and who knows, maybe I can have a positive influence on some of the kids". Sam replied.

"Yes, all very enlightening, but why don't you go and get the coffees in Shivi, these vanilla slices are looking good", Billy said.

Just as they were about to have their coffee and cake DI Morris arrived.

"Amazing timing Mike", Billy said, *"Have you got this room bugged or is it*

your natural built in seventh sense when it comes to cake".

"Just keeping you in the loop, Wojcik has had one session with a psychiatrist and the defence team have arranged for another specialist to see him as well to strengthen their case I guess, anyway, it's going to be a slow job from hereon before this case gets to trial. Thought I would let you know" he said trying to pretend he hadn't seen the vanilla slices.

"There is one for you as well boss", Sam said.

"Well, that's very kind of you Sam" he said, and was clearly in a good mood joining in with the general banter and having a laugh before he said, *"Must move on, have you got a minute Billy for a quick chat in my office".*

"Probably wants to let Billy know what is planned for you two after this week" Dan said after they left.

"Or maybe he's got us a bottle of bubbly" Sam said.

There was little conversation on the way up to Mike's office and once inside he said, *"Sit down Billy, I've got something to tell you in confidence".*

He hesitated for a minute then reached into his desk draw and brought out a bottle of scotch and two glasses. Billy wondered what the hell he was going to say as the whisky was slowly poured out and one handed to Billy.

"It's important that this doesn't get out, I can't stress that enough Billy, but Zac Gold is alive and has been found".

Billy took a sip of his scotch and trying to sound totally surprised said, *"What, I don't believe it, how did that happen?".*

"I can't tell you everything, but he's gone a bit Ga Ga, well a lot really, but information has been secured which proves beyond doubt he's the right man".

"Does that mean the Met have got a chance of getting their stolen millions back then?" Billy continued, *"That Scotland Yard crack investigation team must have done a good job eh? I wonder how they found him Mike?".*

Mike averted eye contact and took a sip of his whisky and said, *"Remember how sensitive and embarrassing this has been for the Met so all this must never come out, or the press would have a field day".*

I don't know the full story, but they seem confident that the stolen money can now be located and eventually recovered but there are apparently lots of legal hoops to go through before they know for sure.

One thing they have found out is that Gold's parents are both dead and he has no other family members. Apparently, he own's a sort of stately home with land which will be worth a fortune which could if necessary be seized under the Proceed of Crimes Act".

"Well, blow me down with your hairdryer, who would have thought they would find this fella Zac Gold after all these years eh Mike?". Billy said, now knowing full well Mike had passed on their conversation in the Bull the other night and feeling chuffed that his plan had worked, and that Mike will have got some credit for the result.

Mike again just looked away, finished his drink and said, *"Cheers Billy, and not a word, eh? Not even to Dan".*

"Not a word Mike, I swear", Billy said, as he left the room and walked back downstairs with a self-satisfying grin on his face.

"What was all that about" Sam said.

"Oh, just telling me how chuffed he is to be finishing his long police career on such a high. Big Brownie points for DCI Geoff Gill as well and even praise for the Chief Constable Keith Dobbs from the hierarchy apparently.

Who knows Sam, maybe your push for Detective Sergeant is a bit closer now and a feather in your cap as well Shivi, if you've got a cap that is", Billy said.

Quickly changing the subject before he had to face any more questions Billy said,

"Listen team, this Friday night the Open Mike Night reopens at the Golden Ball now the repair work has been completed, I know you'll be there with Paula Dan, but if you two have no plans to are welcome to join us, We know you like your music from your quiz nights Shivi, and Sam, it would be a chance for your better half to meet the strange people you have been working alongside for the past six months or so"

CHAPTER 48

Dougie had been making sure that everyone knew it was the grand reopening night with posters plastered inside and outside the pub.

It certainly seemed to be working as the room was beginning to fill up quite early. Little Phil the friendly pharmacist had secured his place on the high stool at the end of the bar and Duncan Disorderly was already on his first drink.

Billy had been in early to check his DJ deck, or his now *"workstation"* was in order and had checked the stage lighting plus the time-honoured method of checking the microphone was working by belting it on the head a couple of times and then shouting *"one two, one two"* into it.

The nights entertainment artists had checked in with Dougie, including Baldy Gary and Whistling Walter to name a few. Billy would be doing his own "filling in songs" while the next performer was ready and Dougie was always on hand to fill in if needed by singing the only song he knew all the way through, *"If I had to do it all over again, I'd do it all over you".*

When Dan and Paula arrived, Jenny was already seated at their reserved table and waived them over and greeted them with, *"I see your big boss was on TV tonight did you see him".*

"No, who do you mean?" Dan said.

"Chief Constable Keith Dobbs, he seemed quite pleased with himself, he was giving a press interview and announced the name of the man in custody for the murder of that photographer called Dorsey ten years ago. He said that this arrest was the result of the hard work and dedication of his cold case review team.

He went on to say that a trial date had not yet been set although the man had admitted to carrying out the murder. I didn't see all the interview as Billy said I needed to get here early, you know what he's like", Jenny concluded.

"I wonder if Billy saw it, I'll go and see if he did" Dan said, but before he had chance to get up Billy was at his "workstation" and was announcing a

warm welcome to everyone and then bursting into his first song.

Within ten minutes the place was virtually full, mainly with the regular "oldies" who look forward to their own sort of Wheel Tappers and Shunters night.

On his debut Baldy Gary went down well with his selection of hand clapping accordion playing and Italian classical favourites. He hadn't missed the opportunity of placing his restaurant flyer on every table plus a stack on the bar.

Whistling Walter was on form introducing some exotic bird species from hot climes that certainly would never be seen in Manchester, and even if they did, they would be more likely to be heard gasping for breath rather than whistling.

During Walter's performance Dougie had arranged for a close eye to be kept on Duncan Disorderly to make sure he wasn't shouting out his usual request.

It had certainly been an enjoyable night so far as Billy put on some music and had his usual brief break. He came over and gave Jenny and Paula a kiss on the cheek and said, *"just the three of you then?"*

"Well to be honest I didn't think we would see Shivi or even Sam, probably not their kind of night", Dan said.

"Not even their generation", Paula said with a laugh.

Just then Dan spotted Sam arriving in the room and looking around, He caught her eye and waived her over.

"Sorry I could make it earlier she said", still a bit out of breath, *"but I had to see what you thought about the news"*.

"What news?" Billy said.

"The Chief Constable's TV interview earlier" Sam said.

"I haven't seen any TV interview, Billy said.

"Neither did we Billy, but Jenny was telling us she saw some of it before she came out tonight".

"So, what's this announcement Keith Dobbs made Sam?" Billy and Dan said at the same time.

"After releasing details of Wojcik's arrest and charge etc, he praised his cold case review team for their work and congratulated DI Mike Morris for his leadership and wished him well on his well-deserved retirement. Then right at the end he announced that further unsolved cases were now to be reviewed by a new cold case team.

About fifteen minutes later I got a call from DI Morris to say that he had recommended to the Chief that I should be considered as a member of the new review team and had also heard that his replacement was to be a quite young newly promoted DI from the neighbouring Cheshire Force.".

"Well, we are really pleased for you Sam, you deserve that, and it will be great for your progress to Detective Sergeant", Billy said. *"Let's all drink to that".*

"Hey, and let's not forget Shivi eh, the experience will have been great for his future career, and we did have some laughs along the way didn't we" Sam said.

The remainder of the night went to plan, well apart from little Phil the pharmacist falling off his high stool laughing at the Roy Orbison impressionist's attempts to reach the high notes singing "Cryin".

All in all, a successful re-launch of Billy and Dougie's "Open Mike Night at the Golden Ball".

Everyone was looking forward to a restful weekend where they could each reflect on what had happened over the preceding several months, and start looking ahead to what life may have in store for them in the future

CHAPTER 49

The two old pals met up at the Crown & Anchor on Sunday for a lunchtime beer.

"Well, that's it Danny boy, you can read and do crosswords to your heart's content now, and get to see Paula more, and best of all I'm really pleased for Mike" Billy said.

"Yeh, I wonder what Mike will do now, did he have any interests outside of a Police station do you know?"

"I know he always fancied himself at golf" Billy replied, *"although from memory he was crap, but at least he can get back to it, and probably a bit of fishing as well. You know Dan, I could never understand why a grown man would sit on the damp bankside of a pond all day long just to see if he can catch some poor little tiddler, only to then throw it back in the water. The only thing Mike would likely catch is piles".*

At that very point Billy's mobile rang. He listened for a minute in silence before ending the call, then with a puzzled look on his face said to Dan, *"Speak of the devil, it was Mike, he wants me to meet him later today, he's got something he needs to tell me, he sounded serious"*

The End

Or perhaps just the beginning of a new chapter in the life of
The Unlikely Evidence Men*?*

APPRECIATIONS

I would firstly like to thank those who took the time to read my first novel ***"The Unlikely Evidence Men"*** *and subsequently expressed their enthusiasm for further writings of the main characters continued humorous evidence gathering encounters, as this encouraged me to write this sequel.*

Amongst those readers were some established authors who kindly gave their time and advice during my early ambitions to put my ideas in writing after my long career as an investigator.

My thanks also to Mediaprint Solutions Ltd once again, for their professional expertise in the cover design and final text format of ***"The Photographer's Final Exposure".***

Finally, thanks to my close knit and caring family for their support and encouragement to continue writing.

Printed in Great Britain
by Amazon

58313739R00129